STONEBIRD

STONEBIRD

MIKE REVELL

Quercus

This edition published in Great Britain in 2015 by

Quercus Editions Ltd
55 Baker Street
7th Floor, South Block
London W1U 8EW

A CIP catalogue reference for this book is available
from the British Library

978 1 84866 717 4 (HB)
978 1 84866 822 5 (EBOOK)

1 3 5 7 9 10 8 6 4 2

Printed and bound in Great Britain by Clays Ltd, St Ives plc.

For Molly Ward, who I will always remember.
And for Jade. She would have loved you so much.

1

It starts at night.

The first thing I do is check my phone. That's what usually wakes me up. The alarm blaring, or a text flashing up from Sam or Dave. But the screen's blank.

I sit up and rub my eyes.

A cold breeze drifts in through the open window, rustling the curtains. I crawl across the bed and reach for the latch. The windows in this house are old and stiff and you have to yank them hard to close them. I try to do it quietly but it still makes a loud bang as it shuts. I hold my breath, listening for any noise from Mum's room, but it's quiet.

Still asleep.

Moonlight fills the room with thin shadows. They drift and twitch on the walls. A shiver runs up and down my arms but I try to ignore it. I'm tired, that's all. It's our fourth night here and I haven't had a proper sleep for days and now I'm having bad dreams and hearing noises and what I really need to do is go back to sleep.

I go to draw the curtains – and that's when I see it.

A huge shadow in the darkness, a flash of gleaming gold.

It sweeps across the garden and blends with the trees, then flies off towards the rundown church.

I shiver again, but not because I'm cold.

I saw the church on the day we moved in. I've seen it every day since, but I've never gone in. It's hunched on a hill at the end of the lane. Some of the windows are boarded up and its walls are crumbling. Mum says it used to look brilliant. She says Grandma used to sing in the choir there when she was younger. Now scaffolding covers one side of the building, and even that looks forgotten. I don't think anyone has used the place in a long time.

But that shadow – whatever it was – flew right over there.

Maybe I'm still asleep. Maybe I'm dreaming.

I yank the curtains closed and scramble back under the covers.

It's not real, I tell myself. *It's not real; stop making things up.*

Part of me wants to turn the light on. Part of me wants to open the door and keep it open so I can see if anything comes in. But Mum says I'm the Man of the House and that means I've got to stop acting like a baby and be more grown-up.

So I take a deep breath, pull the duvet up and stare at the ceiling, counting the cracks.

Waiting for morning.

2

I find the diary the next day.

It's in a box in the garage, hidden underneath a pile of rubbish.

You know how grown-ups always think you're too young to understand anything and talk to you like you're a baby and you want to shout at them but you can't because you have to Respect Your Elders?

That's happening to me now.

'It'll be better than the old house in no time,' Mum says. 'I promise.'

'I just don't get why *we* had to move,' I say, flicking through a bag of old newspaper cuttings. 'It would have been loads easier for Grandma to live closer to us.'

'He's right,' Jess says.

4

Mum stops shifting boxes and glares at us, but after a moment her eyes soften.

'Grandma's lived in Swanbury her whole life. She'd hate to be anywhere else.'

I'm about to say, *She wouldn't realize she's moved anyway,* but I don't want to upset Mum, even if she doesn't care that she's upset me. I liked our old house. I had the best room, and our garden was so big that Daisy could run laps around it. This house is much smaller. It was all right for Grandma and Granddad because all they ever did was sit around watching TV. Plus they didn't have Jess playing loud music through the walls.

'I forgot about this,' Jess says, holding up an old photo.

It must be from ages ago, because I look tiny. It's of Grandma and Granddad with Mum, Jess and me watching a play at their local pub, and –

My breath catches, and I glance at Mum to make sure she's OK.

Because Dad's there too, running to try to make it into the photo before the timer goes off. Sometimes when Mum sees photos of Dad she goes still, and silent tears trickle down her face.

She takes the picture from Jess and her eyes glaze over.

'What a lovely photo,' she says.

Then she smiles, and my whole body sags in relief.

I know we moved to Swanbury so we could be closer to Grandma, but Jess reckons we moved because of Dad. Even though he left seven years ago, you could still feel him all around the old house.

When Dad walked out, Mum said nothing would change. She said she would always be there for us and that she would be a mum and a dad at the same time.

But Dad's gone to live with his girlfriend in Australia and the only way I can talk to him is on Skype. And now we're living here in a dusty old house a million miles away from my best friends, Sam and Dave, and I've got to go to a new school where I won't know anyone and I'll just be standing around all day with no one to talk to.

'Here,' Mum says. 'Help me with this, will you?'

We lift one of the boxes out of the garage and leave it in the storage pile. I asked Mum why we didn't just throw it all away but she said family might want to take a look at it, so we need to hang on to it.

'Have you seen anything you want?' she says as we tiptoe back through the mess.

'Not yet.'

The first thing we did when we moved in was sort through all the junk. Mum said if we liked the look of anything, we could keep it to remember Granddad by, or Grandma before she went in the care home.

I open the nearest box and peer in. More papers, more photos, so old that they're in black and white. At the bottom there's an album in a red leather jacket.

I lift it up and there it is –

The diary.

It's impossible to miss. On the front cover is a pencil drawing, a monster or a demon, tall and black with burning amber eyes. I hold it up so the eyes catch the light, and my heart stops . . .

The thing I saw last night. It looked like this.

'What have you got there?' Jess says, looking over my shoulder.

'Nothing. Just a book.'

I pretend to put it back, then quickly hide it in the front pocket of my hoody.

I don't know why. I just need to have a proper look at it. Mum and Jess have already taken loads of good stuff and I haven't found anything yet. If Jess sees it then maybe she'll want it too.

After a while we stop for dinner.

Mum starts singing in the kitchen as she cooks, and Jess is hogging the TV, so I take the book up to my room. I sit on my bed and turn it in my hands, trying not to smear the shading. The cover's old and battered. It's probably been lying there for ages, because Grandma's been in the home for almost as long as I can remember. And I'm eleven years old – so that's a pretty long time.

I open the cover gently and peer at the first page.

Diary of Margaret Williams, age 13
TOP SECRET

Grandma Williams . . . these words were written by her. Does that mean she did the drawing on the front too? I can't imagine her drawing anything now. I've seen her trying to write her name before and the pen just wandered and wobbled until Mum took it off her. The page was covered in so many inky squiggles that they had to get a new piece of paper.

Thirteen years old. That would make her the same age as Jess. I've never thought about Grandma being a little girl before. She's old and wrinkly and calls me Robert even though that's Dad's name, and she gives me one pound when I visit, unless it's my birthday and then she gives me two.

I hold the cover up to the light. It's a good drawing, part eagle, part lion. The pencil shading makes it look like stone. Like a –

Like a gargoyle.

Suddenly the diary feels weird in my hands. My fingers tingle and my head goes all foggy. I take one more look at it, then slide it under my bed.

3

It's impossible to sleep that night.

I can see it every time I close my eyes. The gargoyle, glaring out of the darkness. Normally I snooze my alarm twice before getting up, but now I can't wait for morning.

'You look like you've been run over,' Jess says, when I trudge downstairs.

She's sitting at the kitchen table dressed in her school uniform. Jess starts at Swanbury High today and has to wear a full-on blazer and everything. They have different periods throughout the day, like science in period one and maths in period two, and you can get double periods like in Harry Potter when they have double potions, and her lessons aren't all in one room with one teacher, like mine always have been.

'Did you have trouble sleeping?' Mum says to me.

'A bit.' I try to smile to show it's all right. I don't want her to know that I always have trouble sleeping here. She's got enough to deal with.

'Sorry, pet.' She puts the kettle on and stares out of the window, mumbling something about the garden looking hideous. Then she turns to face me. 'I spoke to the school this morning. They're looking forward to seeing you tomorrow.'

Tomorrow! I completely forgot. Mum must see the look on my face, because she wanders over and strokes my shoulder.

'It won't be like last time, I promise.'

She means the time I got called Daddy-Long-Legs and had dead fish hidden in my drawer and got invited to Jack's party just so the other kids could lock the door and laugh when I couldn't get in.

'It's a good school. Your grandma used to teach there, you know. And anyway, you're lovely, kind and caring,' she says. 'The other boys will be lucky to have you as a friend.'

'It'll be all right,' I say. There's a smile on my face, because if Sam and Dave heard that they'd smack my arm and call me a mummy's boy. But it doesn't last for long, because kind and caring won't get me very far when the bell rings.

One more day.

One more day until I walk into a class where everyone else has known each other for years and I'll be the only new kid. A class full of staring eyes and secret whispers.

I don't like picturing that, so I sit there in silence, just thinking *orange penguins orange penguins orange penguins . . .* because that always works when you want to take your mind off something. And after a while I can breathe again.

When we finish breakfast, Jess leaves to catch her bus.

Daisy's waiting outside the kitchen door, so I run through to the living room and play with her for a bit. I chuck her ball and she grabs it, brings it back and drops it at my feet. She cocks her head and stares at me, nudging the ball closer. Her eyes are big and brown and her mouth hangs open and her tail's swishing across the floor like a snake at a disco. That's the thing about a dog like Daisy. You can be having the Worst Day Ever and she'll still make you smile.

I chuck the ball again and she scrabbles on the wooden floor and bounds after it –

Then stops. She stops dead still, looking out of the French windows.

'What is it, Daisy?' I ask.

She forgets about the ball and goes over to the glass, whining to go out.

I let her into the garden, and I'm just about to turn back and put the TV on when Daisy stops again, completely still in the middle of the lawn. What's got into her? There's a pub next door and they have a cat that sometimes leaps over the wall. If Daisy sees it she goes crazy. But I can't see the cat anywhere. And Daisy . . . she's not going crazy, or looking into the bushes, where the cat normally hides. She's staring up at the roof.

I know it's stupid, but my heart's beating faster and faster.

I've never seen her like this before, not even when she sneaks up on pigeons at the bird table. Her whole body's frozen.

'What's wrong?' I say, poking my head out into the cold air.

She doesn't look at me, just keeps staring up at the roof.

'What have you seen, Daisy?'

Then she barks. She barks and barks, leaping up on her back legs.

I rush outside, but she's off, running across the garden to the gate, barking louder and louder. I don't stop to think, just chase after her. If she's this worked up, she might try to jump the fence, and if she jumps the fence . . .

Round the side of the house and across the drive and she's going to do it, I can tell she's going to do it. She's legging it closer and closer and –

'Daisy, no!'

But it's too late.

All that's left is a cloud of dust where she kicked the gravel.

I should go back for Mum. I know I should. But in the time that takes, Daisy could get lost – or worse, run over. I rub the sweat from my forehead, then roll over the fence after her.

I know where she's going before I even see it.

The church.

It's ahead of me now, surrounded by bare trees. In my head I picture that shadow again, the weird yellow glow as it flew off. Did it come back? Is that what Daisy's chasing? My breath catches in my throat and I lick my lips. I don't want to go any closer. I want to turn around and run, just run and run without looking back. But I can see the dark shape of Daisy leaping through the grounds. I've got to get her back.

I walk quickly, breathing hard. The graveyard is lumpy and misshapen, as if they just piled bodies one on top of another until they ran out of room. All the gravestones are weather-beaten and broken. There are no flowers beside any of them.

I close my eyes and picture the cold, dark emptiness inside the church.

'Daisy?' I hiss. I don't know why I'm whispering.

Nothing. She's disappeared.

The path leads all the way to the church. There's a small roofed entranceway in front of the main door, where a black metal gate swings on its hinges, creaking and groaning.

'Daisy, come!'

She pokes her head out of the gate, then turns and disappears again.

Great. I let out a sigh and follow her.

The light from outside doesn't reach very far into the entranceway. I can hear Daisy sniffing in the darkness, hear her pawing the ground. I follow the sound and reach out, grabbing her collar.

Right. I've got her. I should go straight back.

But now I'm here, I want to go in. I *need* to go in. Just to see if I'm right.

My heart's beating loud and hard.

Quietly, quietly, I creep up to the door, reaching out to touch the damp wood. I feel for the latch and something tough sticks to my hand. It bends and snaps – *spider webs!* Even in the dark I know it. Without letting go of Daisy's collar, I flap my arms and brush my clothes and clench my eyes shut, and all the time I'm reaching until I touch the cold metal and grip hard and twist.

The door opens with a loud *clunk*.

My heart jolts as something small scuttles past my feet and off into the graveyard.

It's so quiet you can almost feel the silence.

'Come on then,' I say to Daisy, sounding braver than I feel.

I take a deep breath and lick my lips. Then I walk inside.

Dust clouds around me. The early-morning sun filters through holes in the roof, illuminating the aisle and the old wooden pews.

My breath catches as I look up. They're everywhere. On top of pillars and in the corners of the room, stone faces sneering with cold eyes glaring over the abandoned hall.

Gargoyles.

Something brushes my leg and I stifle a scream – but

16

it's just Daisy. She wriggles out of my grip and rushes across the aisle. She barks again and the noise echoes off the walls, ringing all around me.

Then I see it. A small door on the other side of the building, half hidden by a wooden carving. She sniffs all around it, making low growling noises.

'Daisy, be quiet,' I whisper, thinking someone will hear us, wondering what will happen if they do. I glance around quickly, but the place is deserted.

Daisy only stops growling when I get close. I stroke her ears to calm her down.

There's no lock on the door. I've always wondered what kind of stuff gets hidden in churches. Would anything be left if the place is abandoned?

I take a deep breath, then push on the old wood. The door opens easily.

Inside it's so dark I have to flick on my phone to cast a bit of light . . .

I move further into the room, holding the phone higher. A whimper. There's a whimper somewhere, like a trapped mouse. My mouth hangs open, and that's when I realize the noise came from me.

Because it's here.

It's here, right in front of me.

Wide, glowing eyes.

A long curved beak.

Claws sharper than knives, sharp enough to cut through bone.

It isn't just head and shoulders, like the other gargoyles out there. It's bigger than me. Bigger than Mum even, with huge wings that brush the ceiling and powerful-looking lion's legs.

My stomach's so tight I feel as if I'm going to throw up. I can hear my breath getting faster and faster, the blood rushing in my ears. The church was quiet before, but it's so loud now.

Because it's the *same*.

This gargoyle, this big stone bird, is the thing I saw the other night.

It's the thing on the front of Grandma's diary.

Daisy moves in front of me, growling again. Her hair stands on end and suddenly she looks ten times bigger. Her nose wrinkles up and her lips curl back, showing all her teeth. She's barking and barking.

But I can't take my eyes off the gargoyle.

Those eyes . . .

They're flickering, dancing in the darkness.

It's not real, I tell myself.

It's just stone. Just a statue.

'Daisy, come,' I say, but it comes out too quiet. I

glance around desperately for a way out but the only door I can see is the one we just came through and from here it looks miles away.

'*Daisy*,' I say, louder this time, forcing the words out, 'come!'

I try to move but my legs aren't working. The gargoyle's looking right at me, looking right through me, right into my heart.

Come on, Liam! Run!

Daisy turns and bolts and it sparks me into life. I stumble back, out of the crypt, and then I turn and run, legs tingling, heart thumping, out of the door and into the safety of the morning light.

'Where have you been?' Mum says, when I fall panting through the door. 'I've been looking for you everywhere!'

I glance back, but there's nothing there. There's nothing there.

'Daisy got out . . .' I say, breathing heavily. 'She – she escaped.'

Daisy bounds in behind me and starts leaping up at Mum, trying to lick her face.

Mum's expression softens. 'All right,' she says, 'down. *Down*, Daisy. But next time, you have to tell me, OK? I was getting worried.'

'OK.'

She strokes my cheek and smiles. 'Now how about helping me move some things to the loft? I want to get everything done before I go and visit Grandma.'

4

'You don't have to come,' Mum says.

I look at Jess, but she doesn't say anything.

I can tell she doesn't want to go. I don't really want to go either, but it's Grandma's birthday and if no one came to see me on my birthday I wouldn't like it very much. And anyway, I think sometimes being the Man of the House means you've got to do things you don't like doing. Mum gets upset every time she sees Grandma, and I don't like seeing her upset, so maybe I can help.

The care home is at the end of a road called Fair Blossom Drive, but the road isn't exactly fair and there's definitely no blossom. We pull to a stop outside a bare grey building. It doesn't look like a house, even though they use the word home. It's a hospital in disguise. The air around it is thick with the smell of dust and dry

21

flowers. There's a keypad next to the front door, and a button that says CALL FOR HELP in bold printed letters. Mum walks up to it and jabs 2476 and the door clicks open.

'Come on,' she says, 'this way. She's got a new room.'

Jess and I glance at each other, then follow Mum inside.

The last time I visited, Grandma had been shoved in a small room at the back of the building. But they're so old, most of the people in here, and when they die I guess the ones left behind get shunted along into the bigger rooms.

Mum leads the way. Light from the ceiling shines off the polished wooden floor and catches the pictures on the walls. They're the kind of pictures you can stare at for an hour and still not see how they work. Trick-of-the-eye pictures. Jess doesn't seem to notice them though, just walks in front, blowing bubbles with her gum. Groans and mumbles drift on the air from corridors that lead off ours.

Another moan, closer this time. It sounds like a zombie about to grab me and eat me and spit out my bones. I sneak a look into the room it's coming from and see an old woman grinning at me. She has no teeth and her gums are shiny-wet, like slugs clinging to her mouth, and even though I want to stare I quickly glance away.

Demon in Her.

That's what Jess calls it.

She says there's a demon living inside Grandma, eating her from the inside out. That's why she forgets who we are even though we're family, and shouts and screams and cries when we're talking. But looking at that zombie woman makes questions buzz in my mind and although I try to ignore them they keep popping up.

Like, *Does everyone in here have a demon inside them?*

Like, *Does the same demon live in all of them?*

Like, *Where do the demons live when they're not inside people's heads?*

Mum stops outside a green door. She turns to us and whispers, 'She'll be very different to the last time you saw her. The dementia is getting worse quickly. It's hard for her to follow any kind of conversation, and her memory – well, you'll see. Just try to remember who she used to be. She's still in there.'

She knocks in that friendly way you do when you go round to a friend's house – *bap-bap-bap, bap bap!* – and walks in without waiting for an answer.

The thing on the bed can't be Grandma.

It's not a person. It's just sticks and sheets and ghosts.

'Hi,' says Mum, walking towards the bed. 'It's only us.'

'Oh, hello, nurse,' says Grandma.

It's weird how some things stick and some things don't. For ages Grandma used to offer us tea and ask if she could take our coats, even though she can't move from her bed. Now it's clicked that she's not living at home any more. The problem is she thinks everyone's a nurse, even Mum sometimes – even me.

I look down at my shoes, look at anything, but not at Grandma. The room has that old-lady smell, the kind you notice in Oxfam when you look for cheap presents to spend your pocket money on. There are two vases of flowers on the windowsill, one from us and one from the nurses. I can feel Jess beside me and I glance at her, but she doesn't notice, just stares and stares at Grandma.

I take a deep breath, and my heart thuds louder and louder and louder. Mum was right. She's so different to the last time I saw her. Her wrinkly skin sags into the bed and she's small, so small. I reckon I could lift her up, probably, if I tried. Lift her up like a bag of twigs.

'It's us, Mummy,' Mum says again. She smiles. 'It's Sue and Jess and Liam.'

Grandma's eyes flick from Mum to Jess to me. Her eyebrows shoot up and her eyes are wide and watery and they're locked on my face. She reminds me of Daisy when you startle her out of a nap.

'We're here for your birthday,' I say, and I try to smile too, making it as wide as I can and holding it until my cheeks ache.

'Oh!' she says. Her eyes roam the room and settle on the bedside cabinet. There are four cards on it, big birthday cards with the kind of letters you could read from space without even using a telescope. 'It's my birthday . . .' she says.

'I brought you this,' says Jess. She steps forward and hands Grandma a card she made. It's got a pencil drawing of Grandma on it and a banner saying *Happy Birthday* in bright colours. I have to admit, it looks about a million times better than the other cards she has. 'I drew it in art today.'

Long white hands reach up from the bed and take the card from Jess. Grandma holds the paper right up close to her face and peers at it as if she's trying to find Wally. She opens her mouth wide, making a big black hole, then she shoves the drawing in her mouth and chews, biting biting biting. Jess squeals and jumps back, not knowing what to do, and I laugh, even though I know it's mean, even though it's wrong. I laugh and I can't help it.

'No!' says Mum. 'You can't eat that! It's for your birthday.' She snatches the card away from Grandma and holds it up for her to see. The edges are soggy and gnawed. Part of the writing's smudged and wet, so all you can read is HAPPY.

'Oh, how lovely!' says Grandma. She reaches out a bony hand to try to grab the card again. Her mouth opens and closes, opens and closes.

'No, you don't want to eat that,' Mum says, more gently this time.

And all of a sudden I see a fish, a big goldfish with Grandma's face, flapping around out of water, and have to chew on my T-shirt to stop from laughing. Jess shoots me a look that says *STOP MESSING AROUND* and it's in capitals because she looks serious, but I know she's just upset about her drawing.

'Liam's got some chocolates for you, Mum. Do you want a chocolate?' Mum says, changing the subject.

Grandma's face lights up. 'I'll have two!' she says. 'What good's a birthday if you can't have two chocolates?'

I look down at the box in my hands. Mum said a Belgian Milk Selection would be good because none of the chocolates will have wrappers. We brought chocolates last Christmas but they were individually wrapped, and Grandma ate everything, even the plastic.

I loosen the tape on the wrapping paper, so Grandma can easily rip it open. Then I pass the box to her, and she holds it right up to her face.

'Here,' says Mum. 'Let me help you. It's upside down.'

Mum opens the box. As soon as she takes off the lid the smell of chocolate fills the room and covers up the smell of old dusty clothes and books.

'White chocolate,' says Grandma. 'My favourite!' She takes one and pops it in her mouth, and for a moment she's having the time of her life. She chews for about a hundred minutes, then picks another one. She beams at us and the sun shines from the wrinkles on her bone-white face.

Mum pulls up a chair beside the bed. 'How're you doing?' she asks.

Grandma looks at her, and just like that the sun's gone. Her lip wobbles and her eyes rim with tears. She seems so far away, as if she's gazing up at us out of a big cave that we can't go into.

'Get me out of here,' she says. 'I don't like it,' she whimpers, over and over and over. 'I don't like it here.'

Mum grips her hand hard. Grandma's so small and her eyes are so big and they lock on to Mum as she leans in closer. My eyes find Jess and we both look away and stare straight at the floor.

How can she change so much from one minute to the next?

'It's OK,' Mum says.

Tears trickle down on to Grandma's nightgown, mingling with the toast crumbs and jam stains. I rub my hands on my jeans to dry the sweat, and move over to the window. The garden's full of colour, red and blue flowers and the yellow *do-you-like-butter?* buttercups in the grass.

'It's a nice day,' I say, trying to change the subject. I smile again even though my cheeks ache.

'It is,' Mum says, picking up on my thought. 'And look at that garden. I wish ours was half that pretty.'

Grandma blinks. For a second I think she's going to smile too, mention the flowers maybe, or the sun. But she doesn't smile. Her wrinkly face twists and pulls, and she jabs her finger like a dagger in the direction of my heart.

'GET OUT!' she screams, high and cold and so *wrong* coming from someone so frail. 'GET OUT! I'll kill you! I've killed before!'

'No!' says Mum, moving towards her, but Grandma's words ring in the heavy silence and her clawing finger does not waver.

I'll kill you!

I've killed before!

I jump back, trying to find any sign of Grandma in her eyes. My mouth hangs open and I'm staring at her furious face. I try to look away but I can't. A hundred thoughts crash in my mind, but all I can hear is her shouting *GET OUT!* and every thought shatters into a hundred more.

Mum squeezes Grandma's hand. 'It's us,' she says, and even though she's whispering, it's loud – she's trying to hammer it home. '*It's Sue!*'

'Oh, Sue,' Grandma whimpers, blinking, finally turning away from me. I edge away from the bed, behind Jess, trying to make it look as though I'm not hiding. I wonder why Jess is shaking, but then I realize it's me who's shaking. 'My dear Sue . . .'

A nurse pokes her head into the room and smiles around at us. 'Is everything OK?'

No. Nothing's OK. There's a demon inside my grandma and nothing's OK.

I saw it. I saw it in her eyes, the demon, burning inside her, turning her into that thing on the bed that's nothing like the Grandma on Jess's card.

'Yes,' says Mum. 'We're fine, thank you.'

But later, when she turns and takes my hand to leave,

I can see tears in her eyes. She swipes at them with her sleeve, smudging her make-up. She sniffs and doesn't say another word as we march out of the care home, not even when an old man on a Zimmer frame walks up to us and says, 'Have you seen the elephant?'

5

With a loud grumble, the engine comes alive.

Mum's eyes in the mirror do not smile. They're *don't-talk-to-me* eyes. Jess looks out of the window all the way home and doesn't speak. Once I lost her hamster for four days, and no one talked to me until I caught it by making a peanut-butter trap for it to fall into. This feels the same as that. Which is annoying because I can't stop thinking about Grandma and I've got fifty billion questions that need answering.

Has she really killed before?

Or was it the demon talking through her?

Here's everything I can remember about Grandma:

- She had a sheepdog when she was younger.
- When Jess and I used to stay round, she

always made us wash our hands before
dinner.
● She used to cut flowers from her garden to
make displays.

That's everything, and it's not very much at all. There
must be more, but I can't remember. It feels as though
everything we ever did with Grandma was on a holiday
a long time ago, and it's getting blurrier and blurrier
and blurrier around the edges until all that's left is a
big smudge. And the sheepdog isn't even a memory,
not really, just a story Mum once told me when we were
going through old photos.

I don't think Grandma is a murderer. She couldn't
have killed Granddad, because she was in the care home
when he died. And she wouldn't have killed a sheepdog,
because no one would kill a sheepdog, not even a demon.

'Liam!'

Jess is staring at me through the car window. We're
home.

'Get out of the car!' she snaps.

'All right, all right. Where's Mum?'

'Inside. She said it's wine o'clock.'

The time on the car clock says 17.53. Sometimes
different times have nicknames, like bed time and

lunchtime and home time. But I haven't heard of wine o'clock before. I count on my fingers from twelve until I get to seventeen. 'It's ten to six,' I say.

Jess never cries, but I swear her eyes are watering.

Then she blinks and says, 'I know. Are you coming or not?' She storms off, shouting over her shoulder, 'Mum says you've got to get ready for school tomorrow!'

School. It's getting so close.

'I'm just going to get a bit of fresh air,' I say.

I climb out of the car and walk round to the garden. It's so overgrown that it's more like a jungle. The low sun pokes through the trees, making stickman shadows on the grass.

You know when you go to have some cereal in the morning and you see your favourite one in there, Frosties or Coco Pops or something, and you can't wait to eat it, but then you find there's nothing there because your sister has eaten it all and left the empty box in the cupboard?

That's me right now. Not sad, exactly. Just empty.

The sky's growing purple, with red and orange smears on the horizon. Through the bushes at the edge of the garden, the streetlights flicker on. I can't go into the house. Not yet. It'll make school feel even closer.

So I stand there listening to the rustling wind,

listening to the echo of Grandma in my mind. And that's when I realize –

If she did kill someone, maybe there's a chance she wrote about it.

What if there's something in the diary?

Music's already blaring from Jess's room when I get to the front door. I creep through the hall and dash upstairs to my room. The diary's there under my bed. I grab it, then run back downstairs and out of the door.

Before I know it, my feet are carrying me through the gate.

On to the quiet road.

Towards the graveyard.

The other houses on the lane are small and perfect and exactly the same, all the same colour with the same roof and the same gardens. But the church . . .

The light's so low now that the stained-glass windows look dull and colourless.

I try to ignore the cold feeling running up and down my back as I walk up the path and slip through the old wooden door. In the darkness it's hard to see where I'm going, but I can just about make out the entrance to the crypt ahead of me.

My feet scuff on the flagstone floor. The sound echoes in the empty space.

I breathe slowly, in and out, in and out, trying to calm myself down.

Then I push through into the crypt.

It's still there at the back of the room, a dark shape, even blacker than the gloom around it. But something's missing. The eyes. They're not glowing any more.

Maybe my mind *was* playing tricks.

It's only stone. Of course its eyes can't glow.

'You're not so bad,' I say, whispering again. I don't know why but it feels like the kind of place where you have to whisper.

I reach out and touch the gargoyle's chest. It's cold. I stand there, breathing in the damp air. It smells stale.

In here, it's so dark that the air feels alive.

In here, school feels a million miles away.

'I don't want to go,' I say, and straight away I feel like an idiot, speaking to the empty room. *But it's not empty, is it? It's got this great big thing in it.* 'My friends are all back in Colchester and Google says they're two hours and ten minutes away. I know I can call them, but it's not the same. I don't know anyone here. Mum doesn't understand. Jess doesn't want to know. Daisy's the best friend I've got left, but she's just a dog . . .'

I flop down and sit cross-legged on the floor.

It'll be all right, I said to Mum, but I know it won't. Every time I think about school my stomach twists and turns.

I hope the teachers don't find out about Grandma. At my last school they kept asking *How <u>are</u> you?* over and over again, no matter how many times I said I was OK. It's like they expected me to fall apart at any moment. But it's Mum they should have been worrying about. I can't really remember that much about Grandma before the Demon in Her, but Mum can. It must be horrible to lose someone so close to you. Because that's what it feels like. Even though Grandma's still there, she's lost.

Sitting there at the gargoyle's feet, I look at Grandma's diary. The face stares at me from the front cover. I'm one-hundred-per-cent sure it's the same. I get that most gargoyles look similar and I know I probably imagined the glowing eyes, but it's got the same pose, the same face, the same snarl.

I hesitate for a moment, holding my breath. Now that I'm about to read it, I keep looking at those words *TOP SECRET* and thinking it feels wrong. Would I want someone to read my diary if I ever wrote one? Probably not.

But I've got to find out if she really is a murderer.

Holding the pages carefully, I flick through the first few entries. They're surrounded by more sketches. Flowers and buildings and –

And fighter planes.

The War.

Of course I know Grandma lived during the Second World War, but I've never really thought about it. Would she have fought in it too? Could that be where she killed someone?

17 January, 1940

I can hear them every night now.

The planes. They fly like flocks of birds, heading towards Germany and Italy. But they're much louder than birds. When birds sing, it's the sound of happiness. When the planes roar overhead, it's not happiness at all.

I don't know what it is . . .

Before Dad left, he used to take us to air shows every year. I remember the Spitfires soaring overhead, and buying model toys afterwards to build and paint and fly around the house. But that was only two or three planes in the sky. In Grandma's drawing there are dozens.

I read the entry again. They don't sound like the words of a killer. But she's only thirteen here, and there are loads more pages. Maybe somewhere in them, something changes . . .

Suddenly I sit up.

I was so focused that it took me ages to realize.

You know how you can get so used to the furniture in a room that you don't notice when something's different, like when Mum switches the sofas around or changes the side table or moves the elephant statue? Then you squint and you think and after a while it comes to you.

That's how I'm feeling now.

It's still dark. Nothing's moved. But something's changed.

I squint around in the shadows and that's when it hits me – the heat on my back. I scramble up as if I've been burned, even though it's not that hot, it's just warm, like I've been sitting against a radiator.

But there's no radiator at the back of the room.

It's only the gargoyle and me.

And if the warmth didn't come from a radiator, where did it come from?

6

The thing about school is that it always comes round too quickly.

Mum took me in so early that I was the only one there apart from the cleaner, and he didn't say anything, just looked up once and carried on with his work.

'It pays to be early,' she said. 'Especially on your first day.'

But I don't think it does pay to be early; I think that only makes things worse, because now I'm sitting outside reception watching the clock *tick tick tick* closer to nine o'clock, when my new teacher will come and collect me and introduce me to the class.

Mum keeps saying things but I'm not really in the mood to talk, so I say *mmm* and *yeah* in all the right places and try to ignore the snakes in my stomach. I can't stop thinking about the gargoyle. I might have imagined the glowing eyes, but there's no way I made up the heat coming off it . . .

How can something made of stone get so warm?

Just then a woman arrives and holds out her hand. She's got short blonde hair and a wrinkly face, but they're friendly wrinkles, the kind that come from smiling and laughing too much.

'Hello,' she says. 'I'm Mrs Culpepper. You must be Mrs Williams?'

'Yes,' Mum says. 'And this is Liam.'

I stand up to shake the teacher's hand.

'Hello, Liam. Are you nervous?'

'A bit,' I say.

'Me too. We have two things in common already. It's my first day too, you see. I'm covering Mrs Pindle's maternity leave,' she explains to Mum. 'Shall we go and meet our class?'

We say goodbye to Mum, then Mrs Culpepper leads me down the corridor and through a courtyard. The Year Six classroom is at the far end of the school, just past the library. It's right next to the playground and you can still hear some kids out there as they rush towards school.

Mrs Culpepper opens the door. Most of the seats are filled.

Everyone looks up. They're staring at me. I try to swallow but my throat feels thick and useless. Then their eyes slide past me and on to Mrs Culpepper, and in my head I'm saying *thank you thank you thank you* because it's not as bad when you have someone else standing in the doorway with you.

'Stand here until I introduce you,' Mrs Culpepper says. She walks to the front of the class and waits until everyone seems to have arrived, then clears her throat. 'Hello. I'm Mrs Culpepper, your teacher while Mrs Pindle is off. You have a new student joining you today as well,' she continues, pointing in my direction. 'Year Six, this is Liam. Liam, Year Six.' Then she mouths, 'Take a seat.'

I go to the nearest one, but the girl in the next seat looks up and says, 'This seat's saved.'

I move to the one behind it, but that's saved too. A group of kids at the back of the class laugh, and I try to ignore them.

The next seat's free, so I sit down, feeling my cheeks getting hotter and hotter.

Something smacks me on the head and I look down to see a scrunched-up piece of paper on the floor. I pick it up and unfold it. It says: *Starting on the same day as the teacher? You her pet or something?*

First day at a new school and it's already begun.

Ignore it, I tell myself.

'That's quite enough!' says Mrs Culpepper. She glides over and takes the paper from my hand. 'I won't tolerate anything being *thrown* in my class.' She spins around and hurls the paper and I turn just in time to see it smack against the wall and drop into the bin. She walks away from me and over to the boys at the back. 'What's your name?'

'Matt,' says the boy in the middle of the group.

'Do you like disrupting my lesson, Matt?'

'No, miss,' he says.

'Good. I suggest you don't do it again.' She walks back to the front of the class and stands by the board. 'Now, as I was saying, you're going to have to put up with me for the next six months, I'm afraid.'

Quiet. The room's so quiet now.

'In front of you, you have your timetable. This is how the classes will work for the rest of term . . .'

It's pretty much the same as my old school: maths, English, history. There's an asterisk at the bottom of the page and next to it, in photocopied handwriting, are the words 'World War II'.

'As you can see,' says Mrs Culpepper, 'the special focus in history this term is going to be on the Second World War. I've got a really exciting project for you. So let's start with some homework, shall we?'

Homework already? Maybe she isn't so nice after all.

The other kids are sighing and complaining but Mrs Culpepper only smiles.

'Don't worry,' she says, 'this isn't going to be like normal homework. It'll be interesting, I promise. I want you to find someone who lived through the War, and interview them. This could be a grandparent, or a friend of your family, or a neighbour. All you have to do is ask them a few questions, then we'll form a story circle next week and tell each other what we found out.'

'A story circle?' scoffs Matt. 'What the hell's a story circle?'

'Matt, *language*,' Mrs Culpepper says sharply. 'Now, don't tell me you've never made a story circle?' She looks round the class in disbelief. Then she says, 'Yes?' because a girl two rows in front of me is holding her hand so high she's about to fall out of her chair.

'Do you mean like reading? Because Mrs Pindle sometimes reads to us in English. We're on *The Hobbit* at the moment and last term we read *Harry Potter*.'

'A little like that,' says Mrs Culpepper. 'But I'm talking about stories of your own. Stories *you* tell, not me.'

The class is quiet, except for Matt and his mates, who keep whispering at the back of the room. Mrs Culpepper doesn't even seem to notice.

'I can see we're going to need some practice,' she says. 'Form a circle!' She claps her hands and her blonde hair bounces on her shoulders as she points at the floor. 'Quickly, now. That's it! Chop, chop.'

We shove our chairs under the desks and gather cross-legged on the floor. Mrs Culpepper stands in the middle of the circle. She reaches into her bag and takes out an egg, one of those marble ones you see in museum shops for about three pounds.

'This is a magic egg,' she says. '*Only* the person touching the egg is allowed to talk. You're going to pass it round, tell me your name, and something about yourself. OK?'

Uh-oh. Talking in front of the whole class? My mind's moving so fast it feels like it's going to catch fire. I know it's only about ten seconds of talking but no one here knows anything about me and if I mess up they'll make fun of me for the rest of the year.

Mrs Culpepper hands the egg to the girl beside me. I

watch as she takes it and holds it in her small hands. Her eyes look so big behind her glasses. She says her name is Fiona and starts talking about rabbits, but I'm not listening because all I can think is, *Please go round the circle the other way.*

I don't have anything to say. I can't exactly talk about my weekend.

My Grandma threatened to kill me . . .

I look up at a sudden noise.

The girl is holding the egg in my face. Up close, I can see the veins in the marble, clear blue against the rusty brown and red.

'Liam,' says Mrs Culpepper, 'is there anything you want to tell us about yourself?'

My hand trembles as I reach out and take the egg, feel its warmth seep into my hands.

'Um . . . My name's Liam.'

Laughter breaks out around the room and I blink to try to ignore it and my heart's beating and my tongue's so heavy I can't remember how to use it and all the time I'm thinking *orange penguins orange penguins orange penguins*, just to try and focus.

What can I say? Anything that's not about Grandma.

'Did you do anything at the weekend?' says Mrs Culpepper. 'How's your grandma getting on?'

'She's fine,' I say automatically.

Then I think, *How does she know about Grandma?*

Mum must have let the teachers know.

I shift the egg from hand to hand, trying to forget about the faces and the circle.

'It's OK,' says Mrs Culpepper. 'Just pass it on if you can't think of anything you'd like to share.'

I quickly hand the egg to the boy on my left. Matt sniggers. His eyes are thin and mocking, and I can't hold his gaze, so I close my eyes and think of the church, just the quiet church in the darkness.

And the gargoyle.

When I open my eyes, Matt's not looking at me any more.

The marble egg goes round the circle. Mrs Culpepper yelps when it gets back to her. She drops it and only just catches it again before it hits the ground. She holds it up for all of us to see, and makes a big O with her mouth.

'Amazing!' she says. 'It's got so warm. That just shows how good your stories were. Lots of happy memories. And happy memories are powerful things.' She smiles at me and I can feel my cheeks catch fire again. She's looking at me and looking at me. *Why is she only looking at me?* But soon she's smiling at the whole class and standing up and putting the egg back on her desk.

'Next week we will circle up again and tell stories of the War,' she says. 'You all need to interview someone before next Monday. Now – maths!'

7

Over the next few days, I can't take my mind off the homework.

I've got to have something to say, otherwise I'll just be sitting there holding the egg like before, feeling the eyes of the whole class tearing into me.

And that means trying to talk to Grandma.

My heart pops and flutters down into my stomach. Grandma's voice rings in my ears screaming, *I'LL KILL YOU! I'VE KILLED BEFORE!* I close my eyes to try to get rid of it, but then I see her face, snarling and white.

I breathe slowly, in and out, in and out.

It wasn't her, I tell myself. *It was the demon.*

But it doesn't make me feel any better.

Mum says we should always stick to simple subjects

when we're with Grandma. Things like the weather and the colour of the flowers, because they're easy to understand.

The War is not a simple subject. What if remembering it makes her go crazy again?

But there's no one else I can ask. I don't know any of our new neighbours. I suppose I could try asking one of the other people in the care home, but if the demon's in them too then they won't be much help.

Then I have a thought ... if it *was* during the War that Grandma killed someone, maybe asking her is the best way to find out. The homework will give me a chance to talk to her about it without Mum getting weirded out.

'Don't worry about it,' Mum says, when I mention it to her. 'Her long-term memory's often better than her short-term memory.' I don't know what that means, so I don't say anything.

On Saturday, Jess is out with her new friends, so Mum and I visit Grandma without her. Grandma's asleep when we get there. I think we'll probably have to go home because Mum always says it's important for her to rest. But after a moment her eyes flicker open. She looks up at the ceiling then looks around the room and finally looks at us.

Mum says, 'Hi, Mummy,' in this really quiet voice that sounds weird coming from her.

Grandma frowns slightly, and I can tell she doesn't recognize us.

'I've brought Liam to see you again.' Mum moves closer, leaning in. 'Jess is busy today, I'm afraid, but we thought we'd pop in anyway. How are you? How are you doing?'

'Sue,' Grandma says, her eyes shining as she smiles. 'My dear Sue.'

She reaches out a thin wrinkly hand and clutches Mum's arm.

They hold hands for a while, then I step forward and kiss Grandma's cheek. She smiles and her face stretches and the skin pulls tight over her bones, and I know it's bad but I keep thinking she looks like a skeleton.

'How are you, Robert?' she says.

It used to make me feel sad when she called me by Dad's name, but I'm used to it now. I glance across at Mum, but even she looks OK.

'It's Liam,' Mum says. 'He's just had his first week at his new school.'

'Oh, is that right?' Grandma says. Her eyes move from me to Mum and back, then she starts picking at her mouth with a long finger. 'Well, I don't know, nurse. I don't know.'

You know how sometimes things can get so awkward that you don't know where to look? Like when you're daydreaming in class and you snap out of it to realize everyone's staring at you so you spend the next hour avoiding eye contact?

That's how I'm feeling now.

In the sad silence that follows I glance around the room. That's when I notice the flowers on the windowsill. The ones from us are still there and so are the ones from the nurses, but there are some new ones that weren't here last time.

I move over to the window to get a better look. There's a note on them that says: *Thank you for believing in me.* That's weird. Who else has been visiting her?

'Liam's in Year Six now, aren't you, Liam?' Mum says.

I know she's just trying to hammer it home. That's the other thing you have to do with Grandma: if you repeat things over and over again, sometimes they sink in.

Grandma blinks. It's one of her bad days.

Which means I won't be able to ask her anything after all.

Then something changes. Her eyes rim with tears.

'Oh, Sue, they grow up so fast, don't they?'

'They do,' Mum says. Her face relaxes and I can feel the relief flooding out of her.

'How old are you now, dear?'

'Eleven,' I say.

Grandma smiles, and turns to look out of the window. 'A fine age.'

'Liam actually has some homework he was hoping you could help with,' Mum says. She nudges my arm and nods in encouragement.

Here we go.

'What's that, nurse?' Grandma says.

And just like that she's gone again. Mum smiles, but I can tell it's hard for her. She rubs the back of Grandma's hand. 'I was just saying Liam's got some homework he was hoping you could help with.'

'Oh?' She turns to face me again. 'And how old are you now, dear?'

'Eleven,' I say.

'Ah, a fine age.'

Mum gives me a look as if to say, *Go ahead*, so I clear my throat and say, 'Grandma, I was wondering if you could tell me about the War.'

'The what?' she says.

'The War,' I say slowly. 'I was just wondering if you

can remember what it was like living through it?'

Her eyes don't move from mine. Her mouth hangs open and she's so still that I start to think something's wrong. I glance quickly at Mum, but she's just sitting there.

'Oh, nurse,' Grandma says.

Mum squeezes her hand again, but it doesn't do any good because Grandma's wailing now, wailing so loud I can feel it cutting into my stomach as it clenches tight.

I try to swallow but my throat has dried up. I've got so much more to ask, but I can't. Grandma wails until her eyes close and the noise finally softens and stops.

She's asleep. Mum lets out a long sigh.

She looks so peaceful when she's asleep.

'Sorry, pet,' Mum says. 'Maybe we can try again another day.'

We walk back down the corridor. A woman in a blue and white uniform is wheeling a trolley of food to each room. It looks like the same stuff we get at school: powdered mash and horrible-looking meat, but it still smells nice, and makes my tummy rumble.

When we get to the car, Mum turns away to try to hide the tears that are trickling down her cheeks.

'She doesn't really think you're a nurse,' I say.

Mum smiles at that and laughs a tiny laugh. 'I know. I know.'

'Mum?'

'Yes, pet?'

'Have you ever seen anyone else visiting Grandma?'

'Why do you ask?' she says.

'The flowers. On the windowsill.'

'Oh, yes, I was wondering about those too. I haven't seen anyone myself, but I wouldn't be surprised. Grandma's lived around here for a long time. She taught at your school for thirty-odd years. She'll have impacted a lot of lives, your grandma.'

She's quiet after that.

To fill the silence, I go through my options for the War homework in my head.

I guess I could just lie and say I forgot about it.

In my old school I lied to teachers all the time. Not big lies, just little fibs, like when they caught me whispering and they'd say, *Liam, are you talking?* and I'd say, *No*. Lies don't feel like lies when you're in school, because if you tell the truth you get in trouble.

But I think if Mrs Culpepper caught me whispering and said, *Liam, are you talking?* I would say, *Yes, sorry, miss*, because some people you just can't lie to and Mrs Culpepper feels like one of those people.

I'm going to be in Big Trouble. I know it.

Then I remember Grandma's diary.

It might be hard to find out if she's a killer, but it'll be easy to find out about the War. The entry with the planes was one of the earliest ones in there. It won't exactly be an interview, but I'm sure I'll be able to make a story.

8

As soon as we get back, I rush up to my room and dig out the diary.

There are a few blank pages after the one with the planes, but then I find the next entry:

24 March, 1940

I'm not very good at writing about myself but here's everything you need to know.

1) *My favourite colour is yellow (especially yellow roses).*

2) *I am thirteen years, one hundred and sixty-three days old.*

3) *I love peace and quiet (yes, there is such a thing but you have to leave the house for it as*

Mother sings all the time!).

4) *But I also love having my friends around to stay the night (especially when we have midnight feasts).*

5) *I really don't want to move, but Mother says we have to because soon it will be too dangerous to live in Paris. I hope it's not for very long. I will miss so many people.*

Paris?

I didn't know Grandma used to live in Paris!

And all this time I thought we had nothing in common because she has never had a mobile phone and doesn't know what the Internet is and she likes classical music and rubbish books, and I like PlayStations and stories about knights and wizards and dragons.

But we both had to move house at nearly the same age and we both left friends behind.

It sounds as if she really loved Paris. If I had to leave a place I loved like that, I think I'd go home as soon as the War finished. There must be something about Swanbury that she loved even more than France.

Thinking that makes a rotten feeling seep into my stomach.

I can't believe I wanted Mum to move Grandma

closer to Colchester. I know it's really lame that I can't see Sam and Dave every day and go round their houses to play video games after school or football down the rec, but it would have been worse for Grandma to move. The only difference is she wouldn't be able to moan about it because she'd forget straight away.

After that list, the diary entry cuts off, but over the page there's another one:

3 April, 1940

I'm going to try and write in here every day, but it's hard, especially in the evening, because sometimes we're not allowed to have the lights on. That's why our new curtains are big and thick and black, so they don't let out any light.

Mother says it's to try and make sure the German planes get lost when they fly over.

I think you'd have to be pretty silly to get lost in a plane. After all, you're looking down all the time, aren't you? It's like flying above one big map!

Everything feels more real today.

*Elodie and Beth have fled the country already,
and we're leaving tomorrow.*

*Leaving the beautiful streets and the
elegant buildings and swapping it all for
boring fields with cows and squirrels and
ducks. I don't want to go. I tried to tell Mother
that Stonebird will protect us, but she said that's
silly.*

*At least I get to see the cathedral one more
time before we go. I told her I want to draw the
building, but really I want to draw Stonebird.*

To say thank you. And to say goodbye.

I quickly turn the page to see if she's drawn the gargoyle, but instead there's just a picture of some rock.

The ink has smudged. The paper is wavy where it's got wet and then dried.

4 April, 1940

Stonebird's gone!

*I went to Notre Dame today, but he wasn't
there. I can't believe it! He's always been there
before. Mother thinks someone must have moved
him, because of the plane that crashed so close to*

the cathedral. The spire got clipped by debris and part of the roof fell and smashed on the ground.

There's rubble everywhere. But the strange thing is it looks funny.

It's got a sort of marble effect.

I almost ran away there and then. I could have escaped Mother. I could have hidden and stayed in Paris. Maybe then he would come back.

But then another explosion rumbled in the distance and I realized . . . there's no hiding from this.

I hope he's escaped. I hope he's flown away and found somewhere safe.

Like we've got to.

I'm about to read the next entry when Mum calls up: 'Liam, can you come and help me with this, please?'

So I slide the diary back under the bed, careful not to damage the cover. Then I head downstairs and find her in the hall with a huge box in her arms.

'Wedding photos,' she says. 'Thought I'd put them in the cellar.'

I open the door for her and help her down the narrow stairs. It's only when we come back up that I can see she's been crying again.

'Thank you, pet,' she says.

Then she goes into the kitchen and takes a bottle of wine from the fridge. And that's when I realize that wine o'clock is not like bed time or lunch time or home time, because those times don't change. But wine o'clock changes all the time.

9

Later that night I search for 'Paris in World War II' on the Internet and here's what comes up:

- 75,000 people died from bombs.
- 550,000 tons of bombs were dropped.
- The only country more bombed than France was Germany.

That's because the Germans took over and set up camp in France and took all their food and used their money and no one was allowed out at night. Imagine if Grandma hadn't left! She might be dead too and then there would be no Mum and there would be no Jess and no me.

I think about the noise of all those planes flying overhead, and the sirens ripping through the air. I think about the gargoyle disappearing from the roof of the cathedral, and it comes to me.

An idea. A story.

On Monday I take Grandma's diary to school so I don't forget any of the details. I keep it in my drawer through the morning, and then after lunch Mrs Culpepper stands at the head of the class and claps her hands for silence.

She takes a pen and goes to the board and writes:

WAR STORIES

'Right,' she says, turning to face us again. 'I hope you're all ready.' A murmur runs round the class and Mrs Culpepper smiles. 'OK then. Let's form a circle, shall we?'

As everyone's getting up, I rush over to my drawer and have one last quick look at the diary. Then I take my place on the floor. Some people are looking nervous and some are looking bored and Matt and his mates are staring at me, but I ignore them. My knees are shaking up and down, up and down. I try to stop but they just start again.

'How did you find the homework?' Mrs Culpepper says, sitting on the floor with us.

Everyone speaks up at once, trying to make their voice heard.

'It was really fun!'

'My great-granddad is awesome!'

'I'm pleased to hear it,' Mrs Culpepper says. Then she holds up her hand and inside it is the egg. The voices die down until there's quiet. 'Now remember,' she says, 'no talking unless you're holding the egg. OK? Who would like to go first?'

We go round the circle, and people tell stories about Spitfires and making guns and clearing mines. Stories about setting up hospitals inside tents right next to the battle and packing everything up and moving it along every time the army changed its position.

Suddenly I'm worried that my story isn't good enough.

It's not like we're getting marked or anything, but everyone else has something super-exciting to say and theirs have all been real. I haven't even practised.

The egg gets closer and closer. Then it's my turn.

I take it and the warmth seeps into my hands. The words bubble in my mind.

This is a story about how I nearly didn't exist, I say.

And just like that, they're hooked. Their eyes are on me but there's no laughter, no smirks, just interested faces and a silence so heavy I know all they want me to do is say what happens next.

It starts in Paris.

Every night the sky was alive with planes, bombers flying to and from Germany and fighters in the air beside them.

My grandma was there. She didn't know it yet, but it was only a few months before the Germans took control of the city – and in that time it would get heavily attacked.

Loads of people ran for their lives, but Grandma Williams wanted to stay. She loved the city. And she loved the gargoyle that lived there, high on the roof of the cathedral. She thought it protected her.

But the fighting got worse. Distant rumbles and booms came closer and closer. Planes circled in the sky, and every time one got shot, debris crashed down on to the city.

One day Grandma went to the cathedral to say thank you to the gargoyle. Thank you for looking after her. Thank you for keeping her safe. But when she got there, it was gone.

Everyone else thought it must have been moved, but Grandma knew better.

She knew it had flown away.

And that's when she realized the War was coming whether she liked it or not . . .

After school I grab my bag and the diary and rush out into the hall. I can't wait to tell Mum how well it went. I can't wait to tell her about the look on everyone's faces when I told them my story.

Boys and girls hurry past, screaming and laughing and joking.

Matt and two friends are waiting for me in the courtyard. One of them is so huge he could be in secondary school, and the other has thin eyes and pointy ears and rat teeth poking out of his sneering mouth.

'All right, Liam,' says the ratty one. 'How's your girlfriend?'

For a second I wonder what he's talking about, but then the other boy starts singing.

'Mrs Culpepper and Liam, sitting in a tree, K-I-S-S . . .'

'Shut up, Joe,' says Matt, smacking the fat kid on the arm.

Every breath comes quicker and quicker, stinging my lungs. I forget about the gargoyle now and all I can see is Mum. *It'll be all right*, I said to her, and I hoped it would be, hoped it so much that I really thought it would be.

But it's not all right. It's not all right, because Matt and his mates are coming towards me and there's nowhere I can go.

'She's not my girlfriend,' I say, and I hate myself for sounding so stupid.

But it doesn't make any difference.

'Hold him,' Matt says, and the other two rush at me and grab me and push me until I can feel the hard brick wall against my back. 'Open his mouth.'

Grubby fingers grab my face and squeeze my cheeks and I try to clench my jaw shut but they squeeze so hard and I can't hold out and my mouth opens and Matt shoves something damp and heavy and *earthy* inside it.

Retching and coughing, I pull away and spit mud and flowers on to the pavement.

'Tell a story about *that*,' Matt says.

They race off, their laughter ringing off the walls.

I cough and spit and wipe the mud off my tongue with my sleeve.

I don't remember dropping my bag but I must have done because my foot catches on it and I stumble and almost fall.

Grandma's diary has fallen out of it and scuffed along the ground. I pick it up and turn it over and my stomach drops all the way to my feet and stays there squirming.

The drawing of the gargoyle. It's scratched and scraped. It's ruined.

Tears well in my eyes but I blink and rub them away. *I'm not going to cry here.*

My stomach's writhing when I go into the play-ground to find Mum. There are still a few kids running about, still a few parents waiting by the fence, but Mum isn't there.

She's nowhere to be seen.

10

When I get home I dump my bag on the floor and go straight to Jess's room.

I'm hoping she's in a good mood. Sometimes she can be really nice, like when she lets me borrow one of her DVDs, or saves me sweets from the post office. But since we moved, she's been in bad moods more often. And when she's in a bad mood, it's best to be far, far away.

Her music's on so loud I can feel it inside me.

Boom-ch! – boom-ch! – boom-ch!

'Where's Mum?' I yell through the bedroom door.

'*What?*' she calls.

'Where's Mum?'

The door opens a crack and her face fills the open space. A bright pink toothbrush pokes out of her mouth, and she's got a towel wrapped round her hair. The music pounds louder in my ears.

'I can't hear you,' she says.

'Mum wasn't there after school. She said she'd pick me up, but she wasn't there.'

She pulls the toothbrush out of her mouth and glares. 'So?'

'Do you know where she is?'

'No! Now can you go away? I'm meeting someone. I need to get ready.'

'I was just wondering . . .'

But the door's already slamming shut.

I turn to walk away, then hear the door opening again behind me.

'Oh, Liam, wait!'

She runs into the bathroom and there's the *hwwaaaaark sput!* of her spitting in the sink and the rush of water from the tap. Then she comes back and takes my hand and pulls me inside her room.

'I'm sorry,' she says. 'It's just – I want this to be perfect, and . . .' She shakes her head. 'Anyway, come in.'

There's only one rule about Jess's room: DO NOT COME IN. It's in capitals because she only ever shouts it. It's a Very Important Rule, even more important than Mum's old rules like *Turn Off the Light When You Leave the Room* and *Put Your Plate in the Dishwasher When You're Done.*

But Mum's started to leave lights on all the time now, and sometimes it takes days for her plate to go in the dishwasher even though I still put mine in there.

I've only been inside Jess's room once before, when I helped carry her boxes in, and it wasn't decorated then. Now five boy-band faces smile down at me from the blue and pink walls. Jess turns down the music and sits on her bed. You can tell it's a girl's bed because it's got about a million cushions on it and it's as neat as the beds you see on TV, the ones in the sales that never end.

'Sit,' she says. She moves an owl cushion so I can sit down next to her.

'Do you think Mum's OK?' I ask.

Jess opens her mouth to answer, but stops. She closes it slowly and looks at me, tilting her head like Daisy does when she begs at the kitchen door.

'I'm sure she's all right,' she says. 'She's probably just gone shopping.'

'She's normally always there.'

'I know. But – Mum's got a lot on her mind at the moment. Perhaps she forgot.'

'Do you think it's wine o'clock again?'

Jess looks at me but doesn't say anything.

'Well?' I say. It comes out short and sharp and I feel bad for snapping at Jess but I'm so annoyed at Mum. If you say you'll be somewhere, then you should be there, no matter what o'clock it is.

'Has it been wine o'clock again recently?' she says.

'Yes. At the weekend when you were out.'

She sighs heavily. It's a while before she talks again. 'I'll speak to her when she gets back. Anyway, how are *you*? Grandma didn't mean it, you know. When she said she'd kill you. That was the demon talking.'

'I know.' *At least I hope I do.*

The thing that's bugging me is there in my mind but I can't find the words for it. How can you put into words something that you don't understand?

'I can't remember what she was like,' I say. 'I've tried to remember, but she's not there. Not the Grandma from your drawing.'

Jess puts her arm around me and squeezes me. At first I try to resist because she's my sister, but I have to admit it does feel quite good, so after a while I let her hug me.

'She was really nice. Granddad too. He showed me how to make a bow and arrow that you fire with one hand. And Grandma – she loved stories. She used to read to us before we went to bed. *The Hobbit* and *The BFG* and ones about King Arthur. Do you remember that?'

I remember the Shire and the giants and the Knights of the Round Table; I remember the stories. I can hear her voice telling them, but I can't see her face . . .

'It's OK if you can't,' Jess says. 'But you have to know that the Grandma in the care home isn't the real Grandma. Not any more. She's changed. She'll never be the same again. And that's why Mum's so sad. Imagine if our Mum had a demon inside her and had to go to a care home and stay in bed all day –'

'I don't like imagining that . . .'

'No.'

Suddenly there's a crash downstairs.

I rush to the door and press my ear up against the wood, closing my eyes and listening . . . there's the *SMASH!* of something dropping on the floor and the never-ending happy barks of Daisy. Then a voice says, *Oh bugger!*

Mum!

I yank open the door and run downstairs.

There's smashed glass all over the floor and a dark red pool spilling out underneath it. It spreads over the wood and the dirt stains and trickles into the gaps, seeps towards a ripped Tesco bag, which Daisy's nosing around as Mum brushes up the –

I stop on the bottom step. Jess smacks into my back.

It's not Mum, crouching in the mess.

It's not Mum, saying, *CrapcrapcrapcrapNoDaisyohcrapcrapcrap!*

It's not her picking up all the little bits of broken glass.

It's not even a woman.

11

'Hello,' the man says.

Jess tries to get past me, but I can't move. I want to say, *Who are you?* and, *What are you doing here?* and, *Why are you bringing us shopping?* but the only thing that comes out of my mouth is a stupid squeak.

Jess folds her arms the same way she does when you pretend you haven't taken one of her DVDs. 'What are you doing here?' she says, and even though it comes out better than my squeak I can tell she's pretty scared too.

My heart thumps a thousand million beats and I feel for Jess's hand, and when I find it I grab hold of it and don't let go. But if the man was robbing us, he would have run by now, wouldn't he? And he wouldn't bring food with him. I try to think of something to say, but still no words come.

'You must be Liam,' says the man, looking straight at me.

Daisy sniffs at the ripped bag. Her tail swish-swish-swishes behind her. She should be barking. Why isn't she barking?

And then it hits me. Why Mum wasn't there at school to pick me up, why this man's in our house talking to Jess and me as if he knows us.

Because she was with him.

And thinking about her must summon her, because here she is walking through the door with more Tesco bags.

'Hi, guys,' she says, stopping when she sees the mess. 'Don't worry about that, Gary. I'll grab a dustpan and brush. Jess, would you mind taking Daisy through to the sitting room? I don't want her treading on broken glass.'

Daisy ambles over and sniffs my legs. I crouch down and stroke her head, and her eyes make smiles and her tail wags and wags. I could tell Daisy about Matt shoving earth into my mouth and she would put her head on my lap and wag her tail and try to make it OK.

But Mum broke her promise and didn't pick me up from school and she hasn't even said sorry.

She looks at me again and I think she's about to apologize, but instead she walks into the kitchen and dumps the bags on the table. I watch her go without blinking. Sometimes it's hard to say sorry, like when your sister really annoys you and you shove her and she cries and then about a millisecond later you feel like the most horrible person in the world, but if you give in she'll prance around as if she's Queen of the World for the rest of the day. Or when you use the house phone to make prank calls and when the bill comes in Mum says, *DO YOU THINK I'M MADE OF MONEY?* and she knows it's you but owning up to it makes it real.

Sometimes it's hard to say sorry. But most of the time it's easy to say sorry to Mum.

And Mum always says sorry to me.

But not this time.

Jess takes Daisy by the collar and leads her into the sitting room. I still haven't moved from the step when Mum comes back through with the dustpan and brush. Before she opens her mouth I say, 'I looked for you at school.'

Mum frowns, then gasps and drops the dustpan and brush. She runs over to me and takes my hands and pulls me off the bottom step and into a hug, and it feels warm and right even though I'm still angry-but-not-but-actually-yes-I-am.

'Liam! I'm so sorry! I forgot . . . I completely lost track of time!'

I hug Mum tight and close my eyes. If she did forget, then –

'Is there a demon in you, like with Grandma?' I ask.

'What? Oh, you mean have I got dementia? No, of course not! It's just – I just – I've had a lot on my mind recently, and I was out shopping and I bumped into Gary, and we got talking, and – it felt so *good*, Liam, to have someone to talk to.'

'You can talk to me,' I say.

Mum hasn't had a boyfriend since Dad left. Jess is always saying she should go out and find one, but now that this man's here it doesn't feel right. I picture Dad in my head and silently let him know that I haven't forgotten him, even though he's probably forgotten me.

'I know, I *know* I can, darling, but it's not the same. Gary – Gary's going through a similar sort of . . . well, it's just – oh, I don't know what I'm saying. I just need you to know I'm really sorry.'

'It's OK.'

'No, it's not,' says Jess through gritted teeth. Daisy's

dragging her back into the hall, trying to get to the Tesco bag. 'Daisy, wait!' she hisses.

'Jess is right,' Mum says to me. 'It's not OK. It's not OK, Liam.'

Three lines appear on her forehead above her eyebrows. Her eyes start watering and I squeeze her again because I don't want her to cry. When Mum cries, it feels as though I've swallowed a hamster and it's running around inside me.

'I'm sorry too, Liam,' says the man called Gary. He stands up with all the broken glass and shakes the dustpan into the bin in the kitchen. Then he comes back into the hall and stands next to me. 'It's not nice to be left on your own. I'm sure it won't happen again.'

No one speaks, then.

Even Daisy's gone quiet, although her eyes are saying, *Please let me in the bag, please let me in the bag, please let me in the bag.* The only noise comes from the birds outside, singing in the trees.

'Are you OK?' Mum asks.

'I'm fine,' I say.

'Excellent,' says Gary. He picks up the ripped bag and puts it out of reach of Daisy. 'I suppose we'd better be off.'

'Where are you going?' Jess asks Mum.

'Just out for a drink. But I don't have to go if you guys don't want me to . . .'

'It's OK, Mum,' I say again.

'OK.' Her eyes stay on me for a moment longer. 'OK. We won't be very long, I promise. Stay in the house, all right?'

'All right,' I say.

Jess nods too, but when I look at her she doesn't meet my eye.

As soon as Mum and Gary leave, Jess rushes up to her room and slams the door. A few seconds later she pokes her head back over the top of the stairs and says, 'Don't tell her I've gone anywhere. I'll be home before she gets back anyway.'

I run to the front door and press my nose right up against the glass, cupping my hands around my eyes. The back lights of Gary's car flash red as it trundles down the drive and turns on to the lane and out of sight.

Jess pounds down the stairs with one arm through a jacket. She struggles and squirms into it before she gets to the door.

'Where are you going? Mum said we have to stay here.'

'Since when have I ever done what Mum tells me to do?' she says, checking her hair in the mirror.

'Pretty much all the time.'

'Well, if she's going out, then so am I.'

'You're meeting someone, aren't you?'

She's got to be, because she would never act like this normally.

She opens the door and a gust of air washes in. I rub my arms against the cold, watching as she runs outside. *Where's she going?* She can't have that many friends already, can she? At least I've got Daisy. I know she's a family dog, but she totally prefers me. She always chooses me first for cuddles.

I poke my head out of the door, and Daisy comes up and looks out too. Jess is already at the end of the drive and in a few seconds she'll be gone. Daisy stands there, wagging her tail, and I wait and wait in the doorway.

Mum said to stay in, but Mum's gone, and Jess is gone, and now it's just me.

Daisy looks up at me as if she's waiting for something.

I'll be home before she gets back, Jess said.

That means she can't be going very far.

'Do you want to go for a walk?' I ask Daisy.

She leaps up and down in big bounds. I open the door and she practically flies out of it. I follow her out into the evening cold.

12

Pebbles ping from my feet as I dash down the dusty drive.

Birds take off and shoot away from the trees. I catch up with Daisy at the gate, and grab her collar as we go out on to the lane.

The sun's dipping down behind the trees now, making them look blacker than black. *Where's Jess?* I wonder. I spin around, trying to spot her. She can't have got very far . . .

There. Squinting, I can just make her out in the distance. Walking quickly in the direction of –

The church. Has she found the gargoyle too? Something twinges inside me at the thought of it . . . I don't know why, it's not like it's *mine*, it's just . . . well, it does kind of feel like my discovery.

I let go of Daisy's collar and start to jog. Daisy stays by my side even though she's faster than Usain Bolt if she wants to be.

Maybe she remembers our last trip to the church. Maybe it freaked her out too. That's the funny thing about Daisy. She barks this big, deep bark that sounds like *WOO WOO WOO!* but really she's as nervous as a squirrel. Once when she tried to chase off a pigeon it turned around and flapped its wings in her face and she jumped out of her skin and pegged it back inside the house.

'We've got to be quiet,' I whisper.

Daisy understands a lot of words. Most of all she understands *food* and *treats* and *walk*, but I hope she understands *quiet* too because if she gives us away Jess will probably kill me. Whoever she's going to meet, Jess obviously doesn't want Mum to know about it, and that makes it Top Secret.

We run, run as quietly as we can across the crunching drive until it becomes road and we can run faster, on and on until we get to the grass bank. Behind the gate, the church reaches up as if trying to grab the clouds.

Daisy sniffs the grass and her tail goes as straight as a stick.

I crouch down behind the nearest gravestone. It's quite small, but it's enough to hide behind. The engraving says:

CLAIRE SMITH
TAKEN TOO YOUNG
12 SEPTEMBER, 1928 – 16 JANUARY, 1941

I start wondering what could have happened to Claire Smith when she was so young, but all of a sudden Daisy springs forward and dashes towards the church.

'Daisy, no!' I call, but it's a whisper-call, because I don't dare shout.

With a quick glance over my shoulder, I rush after her.

Daisy stops at the entrance and looks back, as if saying, *Come on, then!*

'Is she in here?' I hiss. I squint around, but I can't see Jess. If it was snowing, I'd be able to follow her footprints. Unless she was being Especially Clever and covering up her tracks.

Pushing the door open gently, I peer into the church. Big blocks of light beam through the windows, showing up all the dust in the stale air.

Where are you, Jess?

She could have snuck in before I got here. And if she did . . .

I creep into the church, trying to ignore the smaller gargoyles above me. Past the dust and the broken chairs and the bubble wrap. Daisy sniffs and walks ahead, through the mess.

'Daisy, wait . . .' I whisper after her.

She stops at the door to the crypt and turns back.

I make a *shhh* sign with my finger, and walk up to her quietly. The door's shut. I press my ear up against the wood.

Sudden giggling makes me jump so high I almost smack the low ceiling. Daisy looks back and cocks her head.

There it is again. Giggling and laughing and –

Jess.

Daisy bolts and I go after her, cringing at the noise she's making, willing her to stop, because she's going to run right up to Jess, she's going to give us away. Out of the corner and into the aisle, and there's Jess, at the other end of the hall; she's there with a boy and he's touching her face and kissing her. I almost throw up on the spot, but thankfully I've got a tough stomach.

The boy's kissing her neck now, and she's giggling

85

and smiling and holding his hand, and then she opens her eyes and she looks right at me.

'LIAM!' she shouts, and her voice rings off the walls.

Daisy bounds over to them wagging her tail and Jess doesn't even acknowledge her. The boy does though. He crouches down to stroke her soft head. Jess has got her hands on her hips, which is always Bad News, and now she's marching right at me.

'What are you doing here?' she says.

And I say, 'I might ask you the same thing.'

I heard Mum say it once, and it seems good when anyone questions you. It's like a Get Out of Jail Free card, except this time it only lasts a second, because Jess jabs my chest with her sharp nail.

'I told you to stay in the house!'

'No, you didn't. Mum did.'

'So why didn't you?'

'I might ask you the—'

'*Stop saying that!*'

I gulp one of those loud, slow gulps like you see on TV, because Jess's face is red and her eyes are sharp points and her mouth is one long thin line.

'I was, um –' I say, trying to think quickly, but the only thing that springs to mind is, 'I came to look at the gargoyle!'

Why did I say that?

'The gargoyle? What gargoyle?'

The boy comes over now, with Daisy. Daisy's panting from all the excitement. The boy looks at me and holds out his hand, and I shake it.

'I'm Ben,' he says. 'You must be Liam.'

And Jess says, 'Don't shake his hand! He followed us!'

'I just came to see the gargoyle!'

'So you say,' says Jess, folding her arms again. 'Where is it, then?'

Such an idiot, Liam!

'I meant those ones,' I say, pointing up at the small ones above us.

'Then why are you guarding that door?'

She barges past me, shoving her way through.

'There's nothing here,' says Jess.

And I say, 'What?'

'It's empty,' says Jess.

And I say, '*What?!*'

My heart thuds. I rush into the crypt behind her. If this was a cartoon, my eyes would be as big as magnifying glasses and sirens would be blaring and exclamation marks would shoot out of my head.

Because there are books on the dusty bookshelves

and boxes on the dusty floor and cobwebs dangling from the ceiling. But no gargoyle.

She's right.

It's gone.

13

'If you say anything, you're dead.'

They're the only words Jess says to me on the way home.

Apparently I Spoiled the Mood, so Jess said, *Please just go* to Ben. Then she told me to *Find that stupid dog*, and now we're heading back so *Mum doesn't ruin my day even more than you already have.*

Jess can be really angry when she wants to be.

Once she snuck into Mum's room and tried to use her hair-straighteners and had them on for so long that her fringe snapped right off. I tried not to laugh, but if you've ever seen someone with a snapped-off fringe you know that not laughing is pretty much the most impossible thing in the world. Anyway, Jess got so angry that she burst into my room and thumped me on the arm three times.

But I don't really mind about her because all I can think about is the gargoyle.

You know how sometimes you hear a noise and it's so random that you think you're going mad? Like one day I was on a bus for a school trip and I heard a cow moo even though we were on the motorway, and Sam heard it too and we looked at each other and burst out laughing, but even now we don't know if we really heard it or not?

That's how I'm feeling now.

Because first of all there were the glowing eyes.

Then there was the warm stone.

And now the gargoyle's gone.

I guess someone could have gone in and moved it, but I've still not seen anyone else use the church. And anyway, how do you move a gargoyle that's as big as a whole room?

Then I think back to Grandma's diary. This must be how she felt when her gargoyle disappeared from the cathedral. And my story –

I told a story about the gargoyle vanishing and now it's gone . . .

It was just a story, I think. *Words can't make a gargoyle move.*

Mum's still not back when we get home, so I feed

Daisy and put some water in her bowl, then take my schoolbag with Grandma's diary in it and go upstairs to my room.

Hopefully she's written something else about Stonebird, otherwise the only other option is that I'm going mad.

I sit on my bed and flick through the pages, trying to find any mention of the gargoyle. But after the one with the debris, it's all about escaping the country.

15 June, 1940

I can't believe we're still travelling.

Father drove us all the way to St Malo but it was chaos, people and cars all over the place. The cars were completely packed and most of them had mattresses on the roof to protect them from air attacks.

The officials sent us back through Switzerland and now we're somewhere in Spain. I can't wait to sleep in a proper bed again.

I can't wait to be free.

The entries stop and start after that, and none of them are very long. And there's nothing about the gargoyle.

I flick through more and more pages and I'm about to give up when something makes me stop in my tracks.

13 August, 1940

Today started off awfully.

Someone stole my homework (I suspect Claire as she clearly hates me) and Miss Newbury the maths mistress gave me two strikes from the cane because she thought I hadn't done it.

It's incredibly painful, I don't mind telling you.

But after school I got the most magical surprise. I didn't want to go straight home, and Swanbury has a beautiful church with a huge spire, so I went to sketch some of the graves and the building, and you'll never guess what?

Stonebird was there!

Quite how, I don't know. But it's definitely the same gargoyle. I even compared it to my old drawings.

It has the same pose, the same face, the same eyes. But the really curious thing is that I swear he was never there before – and now he's sitting on top of the roof, looking out over the graveyard.

I wish I could tell Mother, but there's no way she would believe me. And Father's too busy trying to set up his new jewellery shop.

It doesn't matter though. I quite like it being my secret.

Stonebird! Can you believe it?

I knew he was looking after me.

I close the book, and even though I'm sitting in silence, my mind's twisting and turning and all my thoughts are crashing into one big mess.

I know it's impossible for a stone statue to follow Grandma from Paris to Swanbury. It's impossible for it to move at all. But it doesn't matter if it's the truth or a lie or a made-up story. Because if Stonebird really is the gargoyle, then he's our gargoyle; he's our secret.

It's another thing we have in common.

She might be a murderer, I remind myself.

I haven't found any mention of that yet, but that doesn't mean anything. If it hasn't happened by now, maybe I was wrong about it happening in the War. Maybe . . .

Maybe she killed someone right here in Swanbury.

Suddenly the diary's hot in my hands. I quickly slide it back under the bed.

But something doesn't feel right. Before I found the diary I didn't know Grandma at all. Now it's like she's my friend, even if she doesn't know it. The more I read, the more normal she seems.

How could a girl like that ever kill anyone?

14

In the morning I find Mum asleep on the sofa.

Dark marks have spread under her eyes like bruised fruit. There's still a wine glass in her hand, dangling from her fingers. I sit next to her and take the glass and put it on the table. There's a tiny bit of red wine left in the bottom, but it's dried up and scabby. The bottle's empty.

'Mum?' I whisper,

She blinks. Her eyes open slowly.

'My darling,' she says.

'I really don't mind about school. You don't have to pick me up.'

She smiles and looks as if she's about to say something, but her eyes drift closed.

I brush the hair out of her eyes and sit back and

listen to the quiet of the house, all the little noises you only normally hear when you're trying to get to sleep. Sometimes I think houses are like people. They get tired just like we do, and sigh just like we do. They even have faces, sometimes, if you look close enough, with windows for eyes and a door for a mouth.

If Mum was a house she would be a white one, like one of the houses up by the church. Her face is white as a mask. Mum has never liked Halloween, but if she went trick-or-treating looking like this, I think she'd get a lot of sweets.

'She's been like that all night,' says a voice from the door.

Jess. She's not wearing her school uniform.

'Aren't you going to school?' I ask.

'Nope.'

I guess that means she's still not talking to me.

What's got into her? She's starting to remind me of Dave back in Colchester. He didn't do anything his mum wanted him to do unless he wanted to do it too, which was not very often. He played on his PlayStation until after midnight and spent all his pocket money on sweets and hid in the park in the morning so he could ditch school but not get caught.

Mum used to say Dave was a Bad Influence. I think

she was scared I would ditch school too. I stopped spending so much time with him because I wanted Mum to be happy, and then we moved so now I don't get to see him at all.

Jess's boyfriend seemed nice in the church, but I'm starting to think he's probably a Bad Influence because Jess has never skipped school before. It's not like she'll ever listen to me, so I don't say anything, just watch her in the doorway until she turns and walks away.

I don't think she's forgiven me for following her into the church.

'See you later, Mum,' I say, before I head out to school.

'Today we're going to learn about the White Mouse,' Mrs Culpepper says.

'What have mice got to do with the War?' says Matt.

Mrs Culpepper writes *The White Mouse* up on the board, then turns round and says, 'Not mice. *Mouse.* Singular. It's the nickname of one of the Second World War's greatest heroes.'

She tells us about how this lady called Nancy Wake helped smuggle people out of France, and about how she went on top-secret spy missions and even killed a man with her bare hands. Apparently the Germans wanted so badly to capture her that they tortured her husband, only he didn't give anything up.

'She was named after a mouse because she was so sneaky,' says Mrs Culpepper. 'She was so stealthy and quiet that she managed to get away from her enemies before they could capture her. Can you imagine how scary it would be to have Nazis after you at every turn? I'd like you to imagine you're a spy behind enemy lines and come up with a nickname for yourself based on your favourite character trait. But to make it more fun, I'd like you to *draw* whatever your nickname might be, and we can put the best ones up on the wall this afternoon.'

She hands out some paper, then she smiles, which means *get to work*, and there's shuffling and banging as everyone prepares to draw. I pick up the pencil and move the paper closer to me, staring at the blankness.

How do you come up with a spy nickname anyway? It should be easy, because lately I've felt like a bit of a spy myself, sneaking around and trying to find out the truth about the killing. But the more I look at the white page, the more I think I'm never going to be able to start. I wonder if Grandma ever had any trouble with her drawings.

Mrs Culpepper moves round the class, peering at people's work. I start doodling just so I'm drawing something. I sketch and shade and sketch and shade until I hear a noise behind me, and look up to find her frowning at me.

'What's that?' she says.

I look at what I've drawn. It has horns and wings and sharp claws and it's snarling out of the page. All of a sudden my cheeks burn and I can feel sweat on my neck. I guess if I was a spy my nickname would be Stonebird.

'It's – um – it's a gargoyle,' I say.

'Like the one in your story? The one your grandmother found in Paris?'

'Yeah. I guess so.'

She opens her mouth to say something, then stops. 'Is there anything you'd like to tell me, Liam?'

Why is she looking at me like that?

'No,' I say quietly.

She nods, as if deciding something, and taps my drawing. 'A fine creature. You can't get much nobler than a gargoyle. I look forward to seeing this one when it's finished.' She goes to move away –

'Mrs Culpepper?' I ask.

'Yes?'

'What do you mean by "You can't get much nobler than a gargoyle"? What . . . what are they actually for?'

Her face is full of friendly crinkles. I wonder if one

day a demon will move inside her head and turn her into a ghost, into stick-like bones and saggy skin, with fire in her eyes, with tears and hatred.

'Gargoyles are wonderful things,' she says. 'In the old stories, in the days of King Arthur and the like, people believed that gargoyles protected them. Protected them from demons and evil spirits. Kept them safe. But there are those who say they're dangerous, too.'

My heart's pounding in my chest. I can feel it. A rush of images flash in my mind but I can't make anything out. All I can hear is Mrs Culpepper's voice saying, *Protected them from demons and evil spirits*, over and over again.

'What do you believe?' I ask.

'They're good stories,' says Mrs Culpepper. Then she turns away and walks to the next desk, and says, 'Ooh, a dragon!'

When we're done, we hand in the drawings and Mrs Culpepper piles them on her desk at the back of the room. 'These are excellent,' she says. 'I can't wait to have a proper look.'

Then she picks up the marble egg and the room falls silent.

'Now,' Mrs Culpepper says, looking round at each of us, 'we've done introductions. We've done War stories.

Now it's time to move on to stories of your own. Stories that you make up, stories that you tell.'

A shiver of excitement runs around the class.

Everyone loves the magic egg. *Stories stories stories* is all anyone's gone on about. Even the other classes have heard about it, and whenever you walk round school you can hear whispers of jealousy. It's better than doing maths, I guess.

'These can be about anything you like. If you'd like to tell a non-fiction story, a real story that happened to you in real life, you can. But, equally, if you'd like to create something of your own, go right ahead. The floor is yours.'

Mrs Culpepper doesn't even have to ask us to form a circle this time.

We sit and wait for her to take her place in the middle. I think back to the first time I sat here, remembering the fog and my heavy tongue and the egg hot in my hands, remembering not being able to say anything at all.

Just think of a story.

I cast my mind back to everything that's happened this week, from Jess and her boyfriend to the church and –

The gargoyle.

She did say it doesn't have to be about me.

My fingers wriggle in excitement, but I try to keep it secret, because I don't want to look like a massive weirdo in front of the class.

Where's the egg?

There! With a girl called Samantha Potts. Five people away from me.

The gargoyle. Right. But what can I say? I've still got to have a story.

'– and I took my little brother to see him, and all the way I was so nervous. I kept chewing my lip without realizing it. We got in line and we were holding our books for him to sign and all I could think of was that bit in *Blue Planet* when the shark jumps out of the sea in slow motion –'

What do gargoyles do? They sit on castles and hide in churches and watch.

But that's when we're looking at them.

One of my favourite movies is *Toy Story*. The best thing about it is that the toys come alive but only when no one's looking. And even though everyone knows toys are just toys and they can't move and they don't even have hearts, how can we be sure they're not really alive if they move only when we're not there to see them?

'I want to talk about my dog, Bertie,' says a boy whose name I can't remember. 'He's the greediest dog in the world and he begs all the time, but anyway, at the weekend, he ate some paint and started doing blue poos all around the garden –'

Jess says *Toy Story* is a What if? story. *What if* toys came alive when you weren't looking? I like What if? stories. They're the best kind. You can ask What if? about nearly everything in the world, but the best What if? stories are ones where the question is short and simple. What if our headmistress was an alien? What if Daisy could fly? What if dinosaurs came back to rule the world?

All that's going through my head is *what if, what if, what if*, when the egg's passed to me and I can feel it hot in my hands and all the faces in the class turn to look at me. And I just talk, talk without even thinking. It just comes out.

There's a gargoyle in the haunted church, and it's alive.

You might not believe me, but it's true. It's there with the shadows and the ghosts. It's there in the dark.

I know because I saw it. I saw it with my own eyes, two weeks ago.

I ran out of my house and all the way up Church Lane until I was in the churchyard, and the building stood over me. It was so dead you could almost imagine it was alive.

The wind swirled around me and the trees creaked.

It sounded like they were whispering. Probably saying, Don't go in there. Don't go in that church. It's haunted.

But I did.

I opened the door and walked in, and I could hear the ghosts all around me.

Whispering things.

But I knew I had to keep going. Because there was something up ahead.

The gargoyle. There were three claws at the top of each of its wings. Its tail was long and coiled, with a sharp point. And its legs . . . its legs were lion's legs. It prowled the church in the shadows. And it turned to face me.

I stared at it and it stared at me, and I could feel its eyes burning into me, flickering like white-hot moonlight, and as I looked at them I knew things in my head. I knew about its cathedral in Paris. It watched over Notre Dame and watched over the people there and no one looked up, no one cared. I knew it because the gargoyle knew it.

It showed me.

Showed me how it flew through the night to find a new home.

I saw it all when I looked at it.

And I know it saw everything about me too.

It didn't speak, but I heard it. Like when you can

almost hear a dog's thoughts when it's looking at you. I heard it and I knew what it wanted to say.

That it was looking out for me.

That I wasn't alone.

That it would protect me.

I'm staring at the floor, squeezing the egg with everything I've got. Every face is on me, every pair of eyes.

Even Matt. Even Mrs Culpepper.

'What an imagination,' she says.

She doesn't take her eyes off me as I pass the egg to Tilly, next to me, and she keeps watching me even when Tilly starts talking about trying to break the world record for how many crackers you can eat in a minute.

I'd quite like to listen to Tilly because I've tried to break that world record myself, we all tried in my old school, but your mouth gets so dry it's practically impossible. But I can't listen to her, not really, because Mrs Culpepper is still looking at me, and it sends eels wriggling up my neck.

The warmth of the egg still lingers on my hands. I glance down at them, wondering where that story came from. Could I really have just made it up?

When I look back up, Mrs Culpepper's smiling and nodding at Tilly's story, and laughing along with the rest of the class.

15

After school I walk up the high street, past the post office, where boys and girls are jabbering and giggling. They've grown up in Swanbury all their lives. They've got friends they've known forever and they walk in big groups kicking footballs and racing each other and tiptoeing along the kerb and trying not to fall off.

I don't have anyone.

How do you even go up to kids when you're the new boy and everyone already has their friends and they're all laughing and joking? I only have one good joke:

Why do French people never have two eggs?
Because one is an oeuf.

I told that to a girl at my old school and she laughed and her eyes sparkled, and, speaking of world records, at that moment my stomach could have broken the world record for World's Biggest Backflip. But I had nothing else to say after that, and the quiet stretched on and on and then she said, 'Bye,' and ran off.

And that's what will probably happen if I try to talk to anyone –

'Oi!'

I jump a thousand feet in the air.

On the other side of the road, something moves.

No, not something. Someone. Because they're there. All three of them.

'Nice story, Liam,' says Matt, kicking a stone at me. 'Just one problem. You don't expect me to believe that rubbish, do you?'

'I thought they didn't have to be real?' says the small ratty one.

Matt smacks him on the arm. 'Shut up, Cheesy.'

They close in around me and suddenly they're taller than giants.

I'm halfway home. If I could just distract them, maybe I can make a break for it . . .

'Maybe it *is* true,' I say.

They hiss with laughter.

Then I run.

My feet thunder on the road as I peg it up towards

Church Lane and the sound of their footsteps behind me is louder than the rumble of the orcs in 'Lord of the Rings'.

'Get him!' Matt yells.

I bound over the small flint wall into the graveyard and hop across a patch of lumpy ground, dodging between the tombstones and the mounds of earth. The grass muffles their footsteps. I can almost pretend they're not there at all, except –

'Get back here, you little wuss!'

Across the grass and over the wall and into the grounds around the edge of the church. I race up to the crumbling wooden door and only then do I stop and turn around. Matt and his friends are panting by the time they get to me. Matt's eyes are huge and round, hungry. His nose wrinkles, and I can see his teeth.

'Matt,' says Cheesy.

But he doesn't turn around.

'Oi, Matt,' says the other boy, Joe.

But Matt still doesn't turn around.

The others aren't coming any closer.

They've stopped at the edge of the grass bank that leads up to the church.

'Oi, mate,' they say. 'Matt . . .'

Matt scoffs, but finally turns to look at them. He's

like a kettle that's so close to boiling it's rattling and spewing steam. 'What?'

'Something's not right,' says Cheesy. 'I don't like this.'

'You heard his story,' says Joe. 'It's haunted, this place.'

'I DON'T CARE ABOUT HIS STUPID STORY!' roars Matt, rounding on me again.

Back, back, back. Shuffling in the direction of the door. If I can just –

There.

I feel it behind me and step inside, spinning and running across the aisle. My ears strain for any noise as I duck down behind one of the pews, but there's no door swinging, no footsteps, no shouts. No nothing.

A huge sigh of relief floods out of me.

Slowly I peer over the top of the pew. My palms are slick on the old wood.

They've gone.

16

Maybe they did believe the ghost stories.

Maybe they believed *my* story.

The gargoyle faces above me are glaring and the bare branches of the trees are waving through the broken windows, and sitting there on my own with only the emptiness around me it's easy to see how they might get scared.

But there's nothing to be afraid of here.

Unless you count a gargoyle that disappears from one moment to the next.

When I'm sure Matt's not going to barge in, I stand up. Slowly I make my way over to the crypt. Every breath is cold and quick, and I keep glancing over my shoulder to make sure they aren't trying to trick me.

I stand outside the crypt door, listening to the never-ending quiet. The air's heavy and thick with dust. I push open the door and walk slowly down the stone steps . . .

Stonebird's there again, in the dark.

He's there waiting.

'Where did you go?' I ask.

Come on, Liam . . . talking to a statue?

But somehow I know he can hear me. Somehow I know he can understand.

'Is it true?' I say, moving closer, my footsteps quiet on the flagstone floor. 'What Grandma wrote in her diary? Did you really come here from France?'

He doesn't say anything of course. He never says anything.

He's a gargoyle. A statue. He's made of stone.

He can't move.

But he did . . .

And then something else hits me. I told a story about him protecting me, and Matt and his mates left me alone. They didn't come into the church. Or maybe they *couldn't* come into the church.

'Was it you keeping them out?' I say. 'Was it you protecting me?'

Up close, his eyes are bigger than tennis balls. His beak looks sharp enough to cut through bone. The wings are long, reaching out as if he's stretching, and his legs are hunched, ready to pounce.

For a second I see him leaping at me, but I shake the image away.

I look for any sign of where he might have been, but there's nothing. Just smooth, clean stone. He's even in the same position. In fact, it's as though he never moved at all.

'Look,' I say, standing right in front of him now, 'I don't mind that you vanished. I'm quite glad you did actually – I don't think Jess would understand. And she'd probably tell Mum, and then I might not be able to come and see you any more. It's just . . .'

What am I trying to say?

What am I doing?

Even though there's no one else here, it still feels weird talking out loud. If Matt and his mates did come in now, I'd probably die on the spot, and even if I didn't, they'd never let me forget this.

But if it wasn't for Stonebird, if it wasn't for the creepy church, if it wasn't for my story, then they'd probably be beating me up right now.

'I just wanted to say thanks,' I say quietly.

The words die on the stale air and somehow it doesn't feel enough.

I reach up and touch his cold stone face. But it's not cold. Not like it should be. I leap back, scramble as far as I can, because suddenly the image of him attacking me isn't stupid.

He's warm. He was warm before and he's warm again. I didn't imagine it.

And if he's warm, he must be alive.

17

'Where have you *been*? We're going to be late!'

Mum's waiting for me when I get home. Jess is there too. She's fiddling with her nails and paying a lot of attention to the floor. Even though she didn't go to school, she's dressed in her school uniform.

'Why are you wearing . . . ?'

She cuts me off with an evil glare.

'Um . . . Where are we going?' I ask, trying to sound natural.

'To see Grandma! She was asking after you yesterday, so I said I'd bring you along.'

I close my eyes and silently ask Nancy Wake the White Mouse for good luck. Hopefully Grandma will be in one of her happy moods again.

'Are you OK?' says Mum. 'You look a bit ill.'

I think of the gargoyle. Stonebird. I can still feel his warmth on my fingers. I'm not going mad.

'I'm fine,' I say.

Anyway, she's the one that looks ill. Her veins are dark through her skin, and I wouldn't be surprised to see rain fall from the bags under her eyes. I try and make my eyes do smiles like Daisy does when she's happy, and it must work, because Mum's lips twitch, and for a minute her face looks real again.

It makes me remember Mrs Culpepper saying, *Happy memories are powerful things.*

You know how sometimes when you go and visit your Grandma in a care home you wonder if it's really worth it because the next day she won't even remember? But then you realize it's not just about spending time with Grandma, it's about spending time with Mum too, because these are Mum's memories as well and every memory counts.

That's how I'm feeling now. Maybe that's what Mrs Culpepper meant.

'Come on,' Mum says. 'Let's go.'

We get there just after Grandma's finished eating her dinner. A nurse with a trolley full of dirty plates and leftover bits of food backs out of the door. She winks and says, 'She's in a good mood!'

Something flickers in Mum's face. She's got the World's Biggest Smile. She grabs our hands and pulls us in, and there she is, there's Grandma, lying in bed licking bits of meat and carrot and gravy off her fingers.

She doesn't see us at first. When we get closer, she jumps slightly.

'Oh, Sue!' she says, holding out her slimy hands for Mum to hold.

'Hang on,' says Mum. 'Let's just clean you up.' She takes a tissue from her bag. 'It looks like you had a nice meal.'

'Oh, I did,' says Grandma, beaming. 'What did I have, Arthur?'

My heart stutters. That was Granddad's name. My fists clench and I brace myself because any minute now she's going to burst into tears and she won't be in a good mood any more. She'll be in one of her *I'LL KILL YOU* moods, and I don't want to see that again.

Grandma's eyes are wandering round the room now. She looks lost. Seeing her like this makes me feel bad for suspecting her of killing anyone. But when she shouted at me that time . . . her eyes didn't look lost then.

'It looks like roast dinner,' I say, moving into view.

She stares at her hands, at the lumpy bits of sauce as Mum dabs at them. It's on her nightgown too, in

116

splodges over her top. Then Grandma looks up and I can see her eyes grappling with my face. She's trying to remember who I am.

'I've brought the children with me,' says Mum, settling back in her chair. 'I know how much you were looking forward to seeing them.'

'Ohhhh!' says Grandma, and it clicks. I can see it click. The edges of her eyes go all crinkly as she smiles. 'Liam! Little Liam! You're growing up so much! You'll be taller than your mother soon! And where's Jessica?'

Jess steps forward, and Grandma reaches up, trying to stroke her cheek. Jess scrunches her eyes tight shut, but Grandma can't reach, and her hand flops down uselessly on the bed.

Jess looks back and sees me smiling.

'What?'

But I don't know *what*, I just know that I'm happy. It's inside me, lifting me up, spreading warmth through my body all the way to the tips of my fingers.

Once I got three gold stars for a story I wrote in my old school, and it was put up on the wall for the whole term. But even then I didn't feel as happy as I do now, because this is family, this is fun, this is *right*! It's Mum and Grandma and Jess and Me, and we're all grinning for no reason. Grandma's in a good mood and that means Mum's in a good mood, and that's something I haven't seen since we moved house.

'Do you know,' says Grandma, 'if there's one thing we do well, it's family.' She looks round at us, and her eyes are shining. 'Seeing you here – it's lovely. It reminds me of being back up north. I always did throw a good party, didn't I, Sue? In Harrogate . . .'

She trails off, and the silence is long and heavy.

'Oh, Arthur,' says Grandma, and a single tear trickles from her eye down her cheek and her neck on to her nightgown. And *WHOOSH*, there goes all the air in the room. 'Oh, Arthur!' She wails it this time, and now they come faster, the tears, running down her cheeks.

I normally don't cry, because I'm eleven years old, which is double digits. But now there's a watery heat behind my eyes, and I have to turn away. Mum's already there, ready to squeeze Grandma's hand, ready to bring her back to the moment. But she's gone, I can hear she's gone. I know it even though I'm looking out the window at the garden and the flowers and the wooden benches that nobody sits on.

'What have I done?' says Grandma. 'What have I done to deserve this, Arthur?'

'Shh,' says Mum, trying to comfort her. 'Shh.'

Grandma wails again and it breaks everything inside me. She's so small, smaller than Daisy probably, and the demon's eaten everything inside her. Everything but the tears that stream and stream down her face.

Jess is looking anywhere except at Grandma. She catches my eye and turns away, grimacing. Even Mum's quiet now. She's just holding Grandma and whispering in this soothing voice, like she did to Daisy when she was a puppy, howling every time we went to bed.

And Grandma . . .

I saw a frightened horse in a film once. It had eyes so wide you could see white all around the pupils. All they did was look straight ahead. Just stared straight, as if something was coming at them and *fast*. Their eyes were fried eggs. So big and white.

That's how Grandma looks now.

She's scared. She's so scared.

And realizing that, I know what I have to do.

'It's really nice to see you,' I say, turning to move closer to her and smiling the biggest smile I can. And all the time I'm thinking *Please work*, because it's worked before. *Please work . . .*

She blinks. She shakes her head, as if there's something in there she can't understand. *Is it the demon? Can you see it, Grandma? Can you hear it?* But she's looking at my face and her eyes are moving all over it and soon they find my smile, and she smiles too.

'You're so lovely, dear,' she says.

And I can see the smile travelling up her face, all the way to her eyes. She turns to the windows, and the flowers, and the garden outside.

'Such lovely colours,' she says. 'I've always loved yellow. A *happy* colour.'

Just like that, I've saved the day.

When it's time to leave, Mum wraps me in a massive hug in the corridor outside.

'Thank you,' she says, and her words are quiet because she's talking into my shoulder. I can feel wet tears on my cheek, but they're not mine.

'It's OK,' I say.

Our footsteps echo down the corridor as we leave. The pictures flash past and I try to figure out each one on the wall before it's gone, but it's practically impossible, especially the one with the zigzags and the fading animals.

I nearly crash into Mum when she stops at the reception desk.

'Mum?' says Jess. 'What are you doing?'

'Oh, just . . . you know . . .'

Jess frowns. 'What?'

'I just want to take a look at this,' she says, moving over to a picture on the wall. It shows all the staff and nurses and carers who work here. It looks a bit like the team photos in my Premier League sticker album apart from nowhere near as shiny.

Suddenly there are footsteps behind us.

We all look back together, but it's only me who gasps.

Two people are heading our way. One of them is the man who came to the house, the one who broke the wine bottle. The other is a boy who has his head bowed. But even though he's looking at the floor, I can still see who it is. I'd recognize him anywhere.

It's Matt.

He hasn't seen me yet . . .

Quickly, quietly, I shuffle behind Mum, but she's already going off to greet them. *No!* I pretend to be interested in the staff photo. *Please don't see me please don't see me please don't see me . . .*

'Sue!' says the man whose name I've forgotten.

I sneak a sideways glance. Matt's looking up, looking at Mum, smiling at Jess.

Why are you here?!

Of course. *I'm so stupid!*

There's only one reason he would be here, and that's the same reason I'm here. Matt's smile fades as his eyes settle on me and narrow to slits. If he could fire arrows through them, I'd be dead. I look around desperately for backup, but Jess is just standing there twirling her hair and Mum doesn't seem to have noticed.

'Oh!' she says, and she's smiling. Why is she smiling? 'You two know each other?'

Gulp. 'Yeah,' I say, 'but—'

'Well, that's delightful!' She turns back to Matt's dad and says, 'Gary, you should bring Matt round after school one day!'

'Yes!' says Gary, patting Matt on the shoulder. *Why can no one see? Look at him, he's fuming!* 'He's not coping very well . . . I think he'll appreciate the distraction.'

'I am *here*, you know,' says Matt.

'Sorry,' Gary says, with a secret smile at Mum. The kind of smile Jess and I have when Mum says something like *I saw it on the Facebook* instead of just Facebook.

Mum laughs. A real laugh, and for a second I forget what's going on because it's so rare. But then I catch Matt's face again, growing darker and darker by the second.

'Great! That's great. You'll like that, won't you, Liam?'

'Er, yeah, cool,' I manage to say.

No idea how that sounded so natural. What I wanted to say was, *No no no no no no!* But how can you say that

122

when – look at her! She's laughing again. Mum's laugh is the best laugh in the world. It makes her look young and happy and free. When she's not laughing, it's like there's something invisible lurking on her shoulders, weighing her down.

Matt's face tells me he'll like it even less than I do.

In the background I hear words like 'tea' and 'after school' and 'the boys will love it' but the only thing going through my head is, *How is this happening?*

And that's what you call one of Life's Great Mysteries.

18

'Don't think this changes anything,' Matt tells me at school the next day.

I came through the back gate to avoid him because I *knew* he'd be waiting for me, but there he is, lurking against the wall.

'We're not friends,' he says. 'We're never gonna be friends. If you tell anyone about what happened yesterday, you're dead. You get me?'

Before I can reply, his mates come through the gate, laughing and shoving and mucking around. Matt notices them and spits at my feet. He smirks as I step away from the slimy patch on the ground, and goes off to join them.

This huge sigh that I didn't even know was inside me comes flowing out, because he's walking off. No fight, no flowers . . . just threats. I can live with threats. Threats are OK.

If you tell anyone about what happened yesterday, you're dead.

I can't decide if he means I should keep my lips sealed about our parents fancying each other, or about them trying to force us to hang out . . . or about one of his grandparents having a demon like my grandma's.

I suppose it's best not to say anything at all.

It's weird what sad things do to people. Mum is down all the time, and Matt is angry all the time, and me . . . I'm not angry. I'm not sad.

I don't know what I am.

We're sitting in the circle again.

The egg's on its way round. Mrs Culpepper nods when Ruth tells a story about her swimming championships and smiles when John describes the robot he's making with his dad.

But I'm not really listening to them, because next up it's Matt. And look at him. Look at his eyes. Why won't he stop staring at me? His mouth twitches and his lips pull back, revealing yellow teeth.

The egg moves on to him and he holds it and still he's not taking his eyes off me.

'My granddad showed me how to play chess last night,' he says, and finally his grey eyes leave me and roam round the rest of the class. Everyone's waiting on his words. 'But not the normal kind. He plays it through the post with people from Russia . . .'

As he explains it, even I have to admit it's a cool story.

But it's a lie. It's got to be a lie. Because he was at the care home yesterday, just like I was. Everyone's watching him, but they're not *watching* watching him; they're just looking without really seeing. They're letting the words wash over them and picturing the scene and smiling as if they're playing chess themselves.

Matt's knee jerks up and down as he talks. His eyes never stay in one place. It's a lie. It's got to be.

Just like my story. I think back to last week, when I told them about Stonebird. I lied too, didn't I? I had seen him and he did move, he *must* have moved, but how do I know what he did or where he went? I made up a story, a lie, and it felt good.

Maybe all stories are lies, in a way.

But I lied because I couldn't think of anything to say.

I lied because it helped to explain things.

Matt's not helping to explain things at all.

By the time the egg gets to me, I'm ready. Stonebird is in my mind as soon as the warm marble touches my hand. I wait for a moment, tracing the lines of the light blue veins in the stone. I'm not trying to make everyone wait or anything, just getting everything in order in my head.

When I look up, they're glaring at me. Matt and his friends. There's no way he's told them what happened, but even so, their eyes are hot and angry.

If you tell anyone about what happened yesterday, you're dead.

His voice rings in my head, and for the first time I realize I can get him back. Really get him back, I mean. If he went to that much trouble to warn me off, then he must *really* not want anyone to know about our parents.

It would be so easy . . .

I start to speak. *Last night I made a friend . . .* I wait for his reaction. His head snaps round and his hands twitch, as if they're itching to reach out and strangle me.

But I'm not brave enough to do it. I want to, but the look in his eyes is enough to smack the thought out of my head and bring me back to the real world. I would feel great for what, twenty minutes? And then the bell would go and everyone would leave. Everyone apart from Matt and his mates.

His hand moves, a quick thumb line across his neck. Then it's back, resting on his lap.

I pass the egg from hand to hand, licking my lips.

'Go on,' says Matt. 'Who's this friend?'

'Matthew!' says Mrs Culpepper, turning to him. 'Only the person with the egg is allowed to talk.'

'Sorry.'

She scowls at him, then turns back to me.

The gargoyle, I say, automatically.

Out by the church. It was on the roof, sitting in the moonlight. I only noticed it because its shadow reached all the way across the road.

Wings and horns and spikes and claws.

The wind howled around me. Its huge wings reared up. Blood pounded in my ears. I tried to run, but I couldn't move. I looked around for somewhere to hide, for something to help, but where could I go?

And suddenly there it was in front of me.

The gargoyle didn't speak. I don't think it can speak.

But it stared. Its eyes were the size of fists in its massive head, and they shone the colour of the stars.

I still couldn't move – it was like I'd grown from the ground, like I had roots holding me in place. The gargoyle didn't move either. Just looked at me.

Goosebumps tingled on my neck.

Its head tilted sideways and my stomach curled up inside me.

'What do you want?' I said, but my voice was a squeak – I thought it was going to kill me. I knew it was going to kill me. Why else had it flown down, why else was it standing over me in the middle of the street?

'What did it do?' someone says. I don't know who. I'm staring at the egg, seeing the story in it, living it, *breathing* it.

'Shh!' says Mrs Culpepper.

But it didn't kill me.

It turned and sprang up, and its wings thumped and thumped at the air, taking it higher into the sky.

I chased after it, round the bend, down the lane.

Heart hammering, I chased it. Until –

'Let me guess,' says another voice, and this time it's Matt. 'It flew off. *Great* story. You don't expect us to believe this, do you?'

'*Shhh!*' hisses Mrs Culpepper. 'I won't tell you again.'

I need to think of something. A test that will prove I'm right about Stonebird. Something more than just vanishing or protecting me.

But my mind fogs up again. Matt's thrown me off.

The class is watching me, all of them, eyes wide, waiting, waiting . . .

And – um . . .

And it . . .

It landed in my garden. And it just sort of – fixed things.

That's how it ends. With a gargoyle in my garden *fixing* things.

And with the class sniggering around me.

I hold the egg for a moment more, not daring to meet Matt's smirk or the look on Mrs Culpepper's face. Then, cheeks burning, I pass it on.

19

When the bell goes at 3.15, everyone gets up to leave, but Mrs Culpepper calls me over to her desk. She's flicking through the drawings we did the other day. I wait for her to speak, but she doesn't, not until everyone's left.

'You've found him, haven't you?' she says, without looking up.

'Sorry?'

'Stonebird.'

All the air rushes out of the room. I glance back to make sure no one can hear us, but we're alone. Everyone else is sprinting into the playground, eager to get home.

'It's a remarkable picture,' she says, holding up my drawing. 'You have your grandmother's talent, you know.'

How does she –

Then I remember the flowers in Grandma's room. Mrs Culpepper knew about Grandma even before I said anything, and at first I thought Mum must have told the teachers, but what if she never did?

'It was you,' I say. 'You're the one who's been visiting her.'

'Yes,' Mrs Culpepper says, and for the first time a hint of sadness creeps into her eyes. She opens a desk drawer and takes out the egg. 'Do you recognize this? Have you seen it anywhere before? Other than in class, I mean.'

'No,' I say slowly.

Mrs Culpepper takes a deep breath. 'Can I tell you a story, Liam? Believe it or not, it starts right here in Swanbury, when I was a little girl, no older than you. I had a teacher by the name of Mrs Williams—'

I can't believe it. 'My grandma?' I say.

'Indeed. She did the most wonderful thing with the class. Every week, before English, she would sit us down in a circle and encourage us to tell stories. This egg was hers, you see. I seem to remember her telling me that her father made it for her, out of a piece of Parisian rock. At any rate, she was always very careful with it. She called it her magic egg, and everyone loved it, although

I don't think anyone really believed that it was magic. I know I didn't. Not at first anyway. But then, one night, something changed.

'I didn't have what you might call the perfect family. My father – well, he was never the same after the War. Without the danger and the noise and the orders, he didn't know how to live. He was falling apart, Liam, and because of that my family was too.'

I give her a look that says *I know how that feels*, because Mum keeps crying and Jess is skipping school and it feels like we're all falling apart too.

'If things ever got too bad, I used to run away. But I didn't have anywhere to go, so do you know what I did? I turned to your grandmother. She took me in every time I knocked on her door, and we'd sit down with this egg, and she told stories about a gargoyle called Stonebird who had looked after her since she was a child. She said he'd look after me too.'

'And he did?' I say.

'He did. Every time.' She holds up the egg and turns it under the light. 'She gave this egg to me when I finished school. She said I needed it more than her. And I've cherished it ever since.'

That doesn't sound like something a killer would say.

I check Mrs Culpepper's eyes to see if she's lying, but they're steady, locked on to me.

'When I heard what had happened to her, how she was suffering with dementia, I thought somehow I'd be able to help. But of course it's not just her who has to deal with it, is it? It's you and your family too, and everyone who ever held her close in their heart.'

I don't know what to say to that, so I let my thoughts drift back to Stonebird.

If what Mrs Culpepper is saying is true, then –

I was right.

A million questions explode in my mind.

How can Stonebird be real? How can any of this be happening?

'Anyway,' Mrs Culpepper says, standing up, 'I've kept you here long enough. Run along now. It doesn't do to be trapped in school when there's fresh air to be had.'

I get up to leave, but Mrs Culpepper calls after me –

'Liam? Remember what I said. Gargoyles are wonderful things. But be careful. They can be dangerous too.'

20

Mum's waiting for me after school.

I'm so busy thinking about Mrs Culpepper and Stonebird that I almost walk right past her. She has the car with her, parked outside the post office.

'Mum?' I say. 'What's going on?'

'I'm afraid Grandma's in a bad way,' she says. 'I'm going to have to go in again to see her. Jess is out with her friends, and I thought . . .' She stops, and makes the face where her eyebrows shoot up and her mouth zigzags. She's worried about something.

'What?' I say, and even as she opens her mouth, I know what's coming.

Because it's just hit me.

It wasn't random talk, back in the care home. It was real.

'I said I'd drop you round your friend's house.

Around Matt's. Just for a bit!' she adds, when she sees my face.

My jaw's practically on the floor. I mean, ants could crawl into it, it's hanging so low. I *knew* it was coming, but only because it's so mad that it had to happen. I don't realize I'm shaking my head, but I must be, because Mum says –

'Why are you shaking your head? What's wrong?'

'He's not my friend, Mum.'

'Oh, Liam.' She gets in the car and shuts the door behind her. I walk round to the passenger side, but don't get in. There's an electric whirr as the window slides down and Mum says, 'Are you coming?'

Sighing heavily, I flop into the seat, making a massive show of it. I don't even know why – it's just . . . I bet Jess isn't even out with friends, she's probably meeting Ben again, and why do I have to go round Matt's anyway?

'Because you do,' says Mum, and I look away – I didn't realize I'd spoken out loud. 'It's very nice of Gary to offer.'

Why is she so obsessed with Gary?

I wish I could just come out and ask if they're going out, but I'm scared of what the answer's going to be. I guess it wouldn't be the worst thing in the world if

Mum and Gary did get together. He seems all right really.

But if they ever got married, Matt would be my step-brother.

Maybe it would be the worst thing in the world after all.

'I could come with you!' My voice is squeaky and desperate. 'I could see Grandma with you!'

Mum smiles at that, but doesn't say anything. Not at first. I wait and wait, but the only sound is the chitter and groan of the engine springing to life.

'No. Not this time, I don't think. I'm afraid she's in a really bad way. I don't want you to – it might put her out, I mean, having too many people there. I won't be long. I'll be back to pick you up in no time.'

We go to the supermarket so Mum can pick up some flowers for Grandma, then she drops me off at Matt's. His house is on the edge of the village, on a hill that runs down past the sports ground. We pull into a tree-lined drive and the pebbles crackle under the wheels of the car. In an open garage at the end there's an ancient-looking motorbike and one of those old Minis parked next to it. Mum turns the car around and stops to give me a kiss.

'Don't worry,' she says. 'I won't be long. Please be nice to Matt. He seems lovely.'

Oh yeah. Really *lovely*.

I've barely shut the door when the car trundles off and out of the drive, and away.

It's strange that Grandma's got so bad so suddenly. I wonder how she looks, lying in her bed . . . how it's possible to look any worse than she did last time.

When I found Stonebird lying forgotten in the church, I felt sorry for him. But at least he won't wither and rot. Not for a long time. At least he won't forget. What's the point in living, when you're going to forget everything anyway?

Crunch crunch crunch. I walk up to Matt's front door. There's a basketball hoop on the wall beside it, but no net. Squiggly crackly glass makes it impossible to see through the door. I ring the bell, and a dark shape approaches.

'Hiya, Liam,' says Matt's dad, opening the door. 'Matt's just upstairs, playing on his GamesBox, or whatever it's called.'

He opens the door wider so I can come in.

Happy faces grin down from the walls. Photos of Matt and his dad and a woman who must be his –

His mum.

She's got long blonde hair and a smile that looks warm and happy. But if this is his mum, then why is Gary being so friendly with my mum? And where *is* she? Matt's never spoken about her, and she's definitely never there at school. Maybe they're divorced. Or maybe –

I feel horrible thinking it, but maybe she's dead.

I shiver at that.

'Thanks,' I say, snapping back to the moment and glancing away guiltily.

'Feel free to go up. I'm just finishing up a bit of work, so dinner will be a little while, I'm afraid. It's been a bit hectic since . . .'

He trails off and his eyes go foggy like Mum's did for a while after Dad left. I stand there waiting for him to say something, but he doesn't, so after a while I brace myself and head upstairs.

As soon as I reach the landing, I can hear the sound of guns popping and bombs exploding. I knock three times on Matt's door, but he doesn't answer. The gunfire gets cut off by silence though, so I know he's heard me. I can't believe I'm about to walk into his room. My heart's beating as loud as the Xbox. I wait and wait but it's clear he's not going to say anything, so I open the door and poke my head in.

It's pure black, Matt's room, and covered in posters

of cars and rappers. He's sitting on the bed clutching the controller, but as soon as I step inside, he's up and bounding across the room.

He shoves his hand in my face.

'See this?' he says, pointing to the edge of his desk. He runs his hand in a line from wall to wall. 'This is a line. You don't cross it. You get me?'

'I get you.'

'Good.'

He slouches back and carries on playing Call of Duty. There's nowhere to sit, so I just kneel on the floor. Mum would never let me have an all-black room. Or play CoD.

'Is this the latest one?' I ask.

'What do you think?'

His character ducks behind an exploded tank, fires a shot over the top, hides again. Planes roar through the sky above him.

'You're so lucky your dad lets you play on this.'

His mouth tightens, and his thumbs move over the controller in fast-forward flicks. The soldier on screen swaps an empty M16 for an RPG launcher and fires a rocket into the window of a burning building. He sprints out from behind the tank and rushes forward over ditches and barbed wire and –

140

Pat-pat-pat.

Three bullets and the screen's red, and now Matt's throwing down the controller.

'You made me do that,' he says.

Then he falls back on the bed, puts his hands behind his head.

Somewhere I can hear an old grandfather clock. I listen to the minutes ticking away until *BONG BONG BONG BONG* it strikes four o'clock.

The clock reminds me of his story earlier today.

Something rises inside me, and suddenly it's so tempting to ask him, to bait him . . .

He's not going to fight me here, surely . . . not with his dad downstairs.

'Why did you lie?' I say.

'What?'

'Why did you lie? Earlier today, with the egg? When you told your story – why did you lie?'

He doesn't sit up, doesn't even move. 'I didn't.'

Tick-tock, tick-tock, tick-tock.

'You said your granddad showed you how to play chess.'

'He did.'

'Isn't he in the care home?'

That gets his attention. He jolts up, eyes glaring.

'DON'T talk to me about that care home.' He screams the first word, but after that his voice is so quiet I can barely hear him. His eyes get thinner and thinner.

'Why not? My grandma's in there too. I know how it feels.'

'You *don't* know how it feels!' he yells. Then, maybe realizing how loud he's being, he says again, much quieter, 'You don't. No one knows how it feels.'

There's a knock on the door. His dad pokes his head in and asks if everything's OK. Heart racing, I turn to Matt, but he just nods and picks up his controller again.

'We're fine,' he says. 'We're taking turns playing this.'

'All right,' says his dad, shutting the door behind him. 'Dinner's in an hour.'

By the time Mum gets back, the silence in Matt's room has lasted so long it's not even awkward any more. If Jess was here, she'd be bored stiff. She gets bored in about five seconds. But I don't mind being on my own, just listening and thinking.

I still can't believe Mrs Culpepper knows Grandma. It sounds as if she really likes her too. Grandma helped her out when she was in trouble.

I don't think murderers usually help people.

But why would Grandma say she's killed before if it isn't true?

I haven't had a chance to look at the diary recently. If Nancy Wake the White Mouse spy got this lazy, she'd easily have been caught by the Germans. There's got to be something in there. I'm not going to find any proof if I don't look.

'How was it?' Mum asks as we pull away and the lights from the house disappear behind the trees.

It was horrible. The words are there on my lips, but she's been crying again, I can see it. Her eyes are dark and her cheeks are red where she's rubbed them and even though there are no black make-up trickles down them, I can see smudges where she's tried to wipe them away.

'It was OK.'

'Good,' she says. Her lips twitch like she's trying to smile, then quiver and drop back into place. 'Maybe you'll be able to go round again soon.'

'Cool . . .' The word is automatic. But my attempt at a smile is just as bad as Mum's.

21

That night I take out the diary again.

I flip through, looking for any clues, but there's nothing. It's all regular stuff. She talks about her first boyfriend. She talks about finding flowers to put in her hair at the school ball. She talks about playing the piano and watching racing and going for walks along the beach. But I can't find anything to prove she's a killer.

Then I see something that makes me stop.

2 January, 1941

The scream carried all the way across the graveyard. That's the only reason I knew they were there. I ducked into the trees and crept closer, trying to keep out of sight.

Claire and her friends were outside the door. I couldn't see what poor girl they took in this time, but whoever it was, they didn't last long.

She screamed, banging and banging on the door.

I don't understand what's so scary about the church. It's not like there are actually any ghosts. Maybe it's different when they shut you in there.

Maybe it's different when they lock the door.

It's that name again. Claire. The girl who stole Grandma's maths homework. Could all this have something to do with her?

Over the page there's another entry.

3 January, 1941

It was Sarah Potts that they took inside the church.

The news shot round school today.

I really feel sorry for her, because all anyone talked about was how loud she screamed. I thought the whole point of the ritual was to see how long you could last without getting scared, but now it seems as though the only point is to laugh at you.

That's all I could hear when I went to bed last night.

Not Sarah screaming, even though it was loud,
but Claire's laugh. It rang from the walls and
carried all the way across the graveyard.

Locking someone inside a dark church just to scare them? Here I was, thinking Matt's horrible. He's shoved dirt in my mouth and chased me and threatened me, but he's never done anything like that.

It doesn't sound like a ritual. It sounds more like torture.

Even so, Claire was just a girl. A schoolkid. Could Grandma really have killed her? It doesn't seem very likely. But a real spy wouldn't give up on a lead so easily. It's not like I've got any other ideas to investigate.

I slide the diary back under the bed and grab my phone.

Then I Google *Claire Swanbury* to see what comes up. There's something about a baking competition and something about the army and something about a charity run, but there's nothing about a murder.

Jess has said all along that it was the demon talking, and even though I believe her, I can't stop thinking about it.

What if she really was a killer?

But there's nothing in the diary and there's nothing

on the Internet and now I don't know where else to look.

Maybe I'm getting carried away. Maybe the reason I haven't found anything is because there's nothing to find in the first place. I mean . . . Grandma killing someone?

Suddenly the thought makes me feel like the World's Biggest Idiot.

22

In the morning I yank open the curtains to let the light flood in. The sun's so bright that it takes me a while to notice.

The garden . . .

I'm so used to its tumbled plant pots and mountains of red and orange leaves that I stop and stare. The grass is cut and the plants have been put back and the leaves have been cleared. It looks so . . . clean. So *normal*. So gardeny.

'No way . . .'

'Liam!' Mum calls up from the kitchen. 'Jess! Breakfast!'

Mum hasn't made us breakfast in days. I stare at the garden for a few seconds more, thinking how nice it looks with the birds tweeting and pecking at the birdfeeders and the sun shining. Then I run downstairs and into the kitchen.

Bacon. It's the most amazing smell in the world. It fills the kitchen as the meat sizzles. Mum leans over it, shaking the pan to make sure it doesn't stick. The blinds are down. She hasn't seen the garden yet.

Jess comes in a few minutes later, busy on her phone.

'Morning, love,' Mum says.

Jess grunts a hello. Her hair's all over the place and she's still in her dressing gown with her owl slippers on, sliding along the floor like a sleepwalking zombie.

The pan sizzles away.

'Mum?' I say, trying to hide a smile. 'Can you open the window? It's a bit smoky in here.'

She takes the pan off the heat and moves over to the window, rolling up the blind to let bright light slam in. She squints and holds a hand up to shield her eyes. The window latch bangs as she fumbles to open it.

She's still covering her eyes.

She's not going to see it.

Look, Mum, *look* . . .

She turns –

And then she stops.

'Oh my goodness . . .'

She steps back, steps back again, and stares out of the window with wide eyes.

'The garden . . .'

My lips twitch and I have to cover my mouth to hide the massive grin that's trying to split my face open. Jess looks up, her eyes asking the question even though she doesn't say anything.

'Who cleared up the garden?' Mum asks. She turns to face us, still gripping the edge of the sink. Her eyes are watering but she's smiling, and the sunlight behind her makes her look as young as in the photo of her and Dad on their wedding day, stashed in the cellar.

Jess is still looking at me. 'Not me,' she says.

'Oh, Liam!'

Mum rushes over, slippers scuffing on the wooden floor. She comes round the bench and squeezes me into a tight, tight hug, the kind where you can feel your ribs cracking about a hundred times and your eyes nearly pop out of your head.

'Whenever did you get time to do it?' she says. She holds me at arm's length. 'You didn't have to. You really didn't have to . . .'

'I—'

'I love you. I really do, you know.' She turns to Jess and hugs her too. 'Oh, this is just the most brilliant start

150

to the day.' With one last big smile, she practically skips back to the hob to shake the bacon again.

Jess leans in close, eyes narrow. 'It wasn't you. I know it wasn't.'

'Who was it then?' I whisper.

'You're up to something. Why didn't you tell her the truth?'

I can't keep the grin off my face.

After breakfast, when we're walking out the door and Mum is waving at us through the window, I say to Jess, 'I can show you, if you want.'

We're going down the lane, towards the church. Jess has to catch her bus just round the corner from my school, but there should be enough time if we're quick.

'I've only got ten minutes,' she says, checking her watch.

'It won't take long.'

I lead her off the lane, through the thick grass and the fence that crumbles under your hands and up the drive towards the church. It's the same as every morning when I walk past it: old and moody and dark.

'I don't like this place,' she says.

'You came here with Ben.'

'But he's not here now, is he?'

The church door bangs in the wind, cutting her off. It drifts open and creaks closed as we approach.

'It's not scary,' I say.

I lead her to the door, gravel crunching under our feet.

Jess stops, but I push through without waiting to see if she follows me. She won't want to seem more frightened than her kid brother. As we step into the aisle, I realize she's holding her breath. But I don't say anything, because I am too. I don't know what to expect.

Well, I do.

It was Stonebird that cleaned up our garden, I know it was, because that's what happened in my story. And who else could it have been? But it's one thing seeing it in your mind and another finding out with your own eyes that it's actually true.

All the little faces and gremlins around the roof of the church seem more wicked and evil in the light from the broken windows.

'Wait till you see what's in here,' I say.

'Liam . . . this isn't that gargoyle thing again, is it? You're not going to fool me this time.'

There's a sharp bang. A rat scuttles out in front of her and she springs back in shock.

'I don't like this.'

'It's OK,' I say.

She steps back and looks up at the glaring gargoyles. 'You're just trying to frighten me,' she says. 'I'm going back.'

'Jess –' I call.

But she's already gone.

I wait there for a moment, then push through the crypt door, down into the dark.

He's facing away from me, his huge wings curled together like armour over his back.

He's moved again.

And then I see it. Right there under my feet. Mud. Stonebird's trailed mud into the tiny room, all the way over to the window where he's sitting. Mud and grass and leaves.

There are grimy clumps between his toes and under his claws. I glance down at my hands. I can almost imagine the egg's warmth running through them.

How is this possible?

Suddenly I'm glad Jess didn't come in here.

I don't want her to know about this. I don't want anyone to know about this.

I walk closer until I'm standing before him. I reach out a hand that looks so pale in the morning light, and touch his chest, where his heart would be.

It's warm again.

If Stonebird tidied my Mum's garden, then –

'You really are alive,' I say.

He did fly off. He did protect me. He did clean the garden. I've told three different stories and every time Stonebird has acted out my words.

So what if I tell another one?

23

Someone's outside the house when I get back from school. At first I think it's the postman, but then I remember the postman comes at eleven o'clock, not half past three. And anyway, he's got baggy jeans and a skateboard, and I don't think people deliver post on skateboards. It's only when I get closer that I see it's Jess's boyfriend.

'All right, Liam,' he says.

A screech from inside the house.

'I guess you've met Mum then,' I say.

'Yep.'

'Do you want to come in?'

'Better not,' he says, kicking the welcome mat with his toe. 'Seeing as your mum kicked me out and all.'

I laugh, but then realize he might be serious, so I

cover it up by coughing. I open the front door and a wave of sound smacks against me as soon as I let myself in.

'– AND SKIPPING SCHOOL? –' screams Mum.

'– YOU'RE NOT EVEN LISTENING TO ME!' Jess yells.

Daisy slinks out of the kitchen and into the living room. She crawls under the table and rests her head on her front paws. Before I can even take my shoes off Jess is marching out of the kitchen too, tears flooding down her cheeks.

'Jess!' says Mum, quieter now. 'Where are you going?'

'Out,' says Jess, and she's quiet too, both of them suddenly so quiet but it's the kind of quiet that could bubble over at any second, and still neither of them has seen me even though I'm standing right here in the hallway.

'Come back, Jess,' Mum says.

But Jess just barges past me and marches to the front door.

'Jess, you're *thirteen.*'

'Nearly fourteen!' she yells. 'Everyone else at school has a boyfriend. I don't see why I have to be the only person in the world who doesn't have one. He's really nice. Liam's met him. He'll tell you.'

For a second I think they're going to drag me into it, but then they just start yelling at each other again. They're getting louder and louder and higher and higher and I cover my ears to stop the noise. Part of me wants to go and sit with Daisy. Part of me wants to run and see Stonebird and hide in the dark church.

Then all of a sudden everything stops.

I open my eyes.

'What did you say?' Mum says.

She's looking right at me.

My ears are ringing and my mind feels like it's in a million pieces. *Did I say something?* I move my lips, trying to remember any words that came out of them, but I don't like it when people stare and I can feel my neck growing sticky with sweat.

Then the memory comes back.

Something I read in the diary . . .

'Grandma had a boyfriend when she was thirteen,' I say again.

'How do you know that?' Mum says. Her face is as still as a stone mask and I can't tell if she's angry or upset any more. 'I didn't even know that.'

And that's when I know I can't keep Grandma's diary a secret any longer. I could try to think up a story but it wouldn't work, not now, not with my head ringing like this.

'I read it in her diary,' I say.

'Her diary?'

'I found it when we were sorting stuff. It was in a box in the garage.'

'And you didn't think to tell me about it?' Mum turns to Jess and says, 'Did you know about this?'

Jess shakes her head.

You know how there are two types of crying and one can make you a bit annoyed and one can make you really sad? Like when you hear a baby crying on a train and it's the loudest thing ever and all you want to do is get off to find some peace and quiet, but if you see someone crying silently with tears trickling slowly down their cheeks it makes you feel like you're a domino falling over on the spot?

That's how I'm feeling now – like a great big domino falling on to my back.

Later that night I'm lying in bed thinking, *It's all my fault*.

I gave Mum the diary but she's still downstairs and it's been wine o'clock for a while now. Jess is in her room with the music blaring and she's probably crying too.

This morning everything was perfect. Mum was so happy she could have danced around the house, and even Jess was OK. Now everything's falling apart and every single bit of it is because of me.

But I'm the Man of the House and that means I've got to try to put things right.

The trouble is, how do you put things right when there's so much to fix? I wonder if Nancy Wake the White Mouse ever felt like this when she was dodging Nazis and smuggling people out of France.

Then it hits me.

Stonebird.

If he sorted out Mum's garden just because I told a story about it, maybe he can help me again now. But that garden story was so embarrassing! I didn't exactly plan on saying it. It just came out. And what if it doesn't work this time?

Even so, the thought lights something inside me that sparks and burns and makes me want to get back to school as soon as possible.

I pull out a notebook and grab a pen to make a list of things to fix, and this is what it says:

- Help Mum deal with all the rubbish stuff that's happening.

- Stop Jess from bunking and help her make up with Mum.
- Stop Matt bullying me once and for all.

Now all I have to do is think up some really good stories.

24

The next time we sit in the story circle, I'm ready.

I want to listen to the other stories, but my head is whirring and I can't focus. I'm just waiting for the egg to get to me.

I take it in my hands and hold it up, thinking of the gargoyle, thinking of Stonebird, but most of all thinking about Mum. The words are on my tongue even before I really know what I'm going to say, and all I have to do is open my mouth.

It was a cold night, I say, *and the gargoyle was stirring.*

It crouched on the church, waiting in the moonlight, listening to the wind and the trees, listening to the sounds that only gargoyles can hear.

The sounds of sorrow.

The sounds of fear.

The sounds of wishes and hopes and dreams.

It was quieter here than in its old home. Notre Dame was loud. There were too many people, too many demons, too many things to fix.

Here it was easier to focus.

The gargoyle spread its wings and leaped from the church to fly over the city.

That was when it heard sadness and tears and really loud terrible music, and it knew that there was one family that needed help more than any other . . .

I don't name any names and I don't just talk about Mum and Jess, because that wouldn't feel right and would probably sound a bit weird, so I mention some other people in the village, people all the other kids would know about.

Like Wheelbarrow Will, the old man who always takes his wheelbarrow to the post office to collect his groceries and his newspaper. Wherever he goes, he whispers to himself.

And Mrs Rowden, the lady who stares at you when you go past her house.

You know how some people can seem really weird when you see them, especially if they do strange things like take wheelbarrows to the shops or stare out of the window all the time? I was thinking about it and what I reckon is this: they're probably no more weird than anyone else, because we're all weird in different ways. And there may be a really sad reason why they do those things, like the way wine o'clock keeps happening in our house because Mum loves Grandma loads but Grandma's disappearing more and more every day.

That's why I put them all in my story, so Stonebird can help them.

The rest of the day goes really slowly because all I want to do is get home and see if the story's worked.

Mrs Culpepper's telling us about another hero of the War. He's called Oskar Schindler, but that's all I remember because her words are going in one side of my head and out of the other without sticking.

The only thing that does stick is the potato.

At lunch, Matt walks past my table and flicks some mash at me. It lands on my lap with a wet thud. I flick it off on to the floor, but when I look up he's still there.

'When are you going to stop telling stupid stories?' he says.

'When are you going to leave me alone?' I say.

He glares at me, then drops another splodge of potato and this time it lands on my shoe. 'Oops,' he says. Then he saunters off laughing and calls over his shoulder, 'Could be a while!'

A couple of other Year Sixes see me scraping the potato off my foot and glance away, pretending not to have noticed. Sometimes I think that's more annoying than Matt being a bully in the first place. I know I should tell someone, but I don't. Maybe that makes me as bad as them.

I'm not hungry any more, so I leave the rest of my food and sit in the classroom until the end of lunch.

All through the rest of the day I keep looking up at the clock every few minutes.

Finally home time comes and I rush off as fast as possible, just in case Matt's planning anything else.

When I get home, there's a note from Mum stuck to the fridge:

Gone out with Gary, back later
Pizza in the fridge – love Mum

Jess gets home ten minutes later and she's got the World's Biggest Scowl on her face. 'I got a text from Mum,' she says. 'I've got to babysit you. You're ruining my evening, just so you know.'

'I don't need babysitting,' I say.

'That's what I said.'

Daisy bounds up to us but Jess doesn't even say hello, which isn't very nice because it's not like Daisy's done anything wrong – she doesn't know what's going on; she's just glad to see us.

I go upstairs and lie in bed watching TV. After a while my eyes start to drift closed. I try and fight it but they're too heavy, and before I know it I'm falling into darkness.

I'm on my back in a river and the water's pulling me away, pulling me off towards the orange horizon. The sun's melting into the dark, dark ground and the birds are singing goodbye to the day and all I know is that I could stay here forever, just stay here and forget about the world –

Something's here.

That's the thought that wakes me up.

Something's here. Something's in my room.

I don't move. I stay right there and look across the room, and even though it's dark I can see it. My heart flips in my chest –

'Stonebird,' I say.

'Liam,' says a voice.

And I'm thinking, *That's weird.* Stonebird doesn't speak.

'My dear Liam,' says the voice again, and now I do sit up. Because it's not the gargoyle standing over me. It's –

'Mum?' I say. 'It's OK,' Mum says. 'I didn't mean to wake you.'

'I'm sorry about the diary. I should have told you about it.'

'Don't apologize,' she says, stroking my head. 'It's me who should be sorry. Of course you want to know more about your grandma. It's only natural. Although, now that you mention it, do you still have the entry from 16 January, 1941?'

'What do you mean?' I ask.

'It's just it's not there. It's gone. Ripped out.'

What?

I rub my eyes, trying to shake off the foggy feeling.

A torn-out page? How could I have missed that! Surely Grandma wouldn't rip a page out of her diary . . . unless there was something she really wanted to hide . . .

'I never realized,' I say, trying to remember something – anything – about that January in the diary. But I can't think. Already my eyes are drifting closed again.

'Not to worry, my lovely boy. Sleep well. I'll see you in the morning.'

She goes to draw the curtains and just before she does, just before the room is plunged into darkness, I'm sure I can see an amber glow through the window.

25

The first thing I do the next morning is rush to the window.

Actually, that's not true. The first thing I do is turn off the alarm and the second thing I do is yawn and the third thing I do is stretch. But then I remember my story. I remember the orange glow in the night and I leap up and throw open the window and look out.

The amber light is gone.

Just like that, my insides crumple up.

It must have been too much to ask for. Maybe Stonebird's like the genie in Aladdin and can't change anything to do with the heart. Maybe I made my list and told my story for nothing.

I'm about to close the window when something in the garden catches my eye.

He's there.

Stonebird's out there, on the grass.

'It worked,' I whisper, and I'm shaking my head now because I can't believe it. 'It worked!' I say, louder this time, and I don't care if anyone hears me and I don't care if I sound crazy, because it worked it worked it worked!

Stonebird looks up at me, and I stare right back.

I mouth, *Thank you.*

Then he turns, and leaps up over the bushes and away into the early-morning light.

My stomach fizzes as I skip down the stairs.

There are voices coming from the kitchen. I guess that means Mum and Jess are talking again. In fact, it turns out they're even laughing over Grandma's diary, reading about her first boyfriend.

'Rupert?' says Jess, choking on her Coco Pops. 'I didn't think anyone was actually called Rupert.'

Even though I'm bouncing with happiness after seeing Stonebird, I can't take my eyes off the diary. The torn-out page can only mean one thing. But to be sure, I've got to go back to those January entries. And that means getting it away from Mum and Jess.

Before I leave for school, Mum drags me into a hug.

'I really am sorry about yesterday,' she says. 'I don't know what came over me.'

'It's OK, Mum.'

'Jess is sorry too, she just doesn't know how to say it. It's going to be a weird time for her at the moment. You know, *hormones* and all.'

I don't know what that means, but I smile and hug her again and head out of the door.

I still can't believe Stonebird came in the night. That's four times now. Four stories I've told and four times it's acted out my words. That must be why Mum woke me up. She's in a better mood than she has been for ages, and she's talking to Jess too.

And it's all because of Stonebird.

It's all because of –

Because of me.

I'm in such a happy mood that there's only one thing that can ruin it.

So guess who's waiting for me in the courtyard outside school?

Matt, with Cheesy and Joe.

I try to pretend I haven't seen them and walk straight up to the double doors, but Cheesy blocks my way.

'Don't think so,' he says, laughing his fake laugh, sending flecks of spit flying from his mouth.

I turn around to go back the other way, but now Joe's blocking the path.

Slow breaths, I tell myself. *Just take slow breaths.*

But it's hard to breathe when it feels like your lungs are in your throat.

I glance around for any teachers, trying not to look scared. But they'll be inside by now. Maybe there's a window nearby . . . if I can just get into the right position, someone will have to see us. The trouble is, Matt's mates aren't giving me any space to move.

Then I hear another voice and turn to see something that makes me swell with hope –

'Boys,' says Mr Hill, the Year Four teacher, walking down the path towards reception.

But he's not looking, he's not looking, not properly anyway, he's just striding off and soon I'll be on my own again . . .

'Sir!' I say, trying to move towards him.

'I hope you're on your way to your lessons?' he says.

'Definitely,' Matt says, and his arm's around me now. He's got my shoulders and he's leading me away, around the corner to the back of the school grounds. 'That's exactly where we're going.'

'Good, good,' says the far-off voice of Mr Hill.

Then he's out of sight.

But worse – so are we.

Matt's voice is loud and harsh in my ear. 'You know better than that, Liam.'

'Yeah,' says Joe. 'That could have been a problem.'

'Shut up,' Matt spits.

They finally stop dragging me along. I look around and my first thought is that they've taken me away from school. We're not in the big playground and we're not in the small playground. But we can't have left the school grounds. We weren't walking for that long. Ahead of us there's a glass door that looks as if it leads to the library. And beside us –

Beside us is a pond.

'What are you doing?' I say. 'We're going to be late.'

I know Mrs Culpepper probably won't mind because she never tells anyone off, not really, but it's the first thing that comes to my mind and I'm hoping it's enough to make them stall. If I can get them to hesitate just for a second, maybe I can escape.

'I didn't lie,' Matt says. He steps back and the look on his face makes my stomach curl up. 'I said we're going to our lessons, and here we are. This is the most important lesson you'll learn all day: always bring a towel to school.'

He grabs my shoulder and leans in close, dropping

his voice so the others can't hear him. 'Tell your mum to stay away from my dad,' he hisses.

Then he shoves me.

I stumble back. The pond rears up.

It comes at me in slow motion, but there's nothing I can do to stop it –

Splash.

The world vanishes in a rush of bubbles.

I shut my eyes tight as I plunge into the water.

Blindly I reach out as weeds tangle round me. My nose stings and already my lungs are burning. I need to find the bottom, but I don't dare open my eyes.

Then my legs scrape something hard and I kick off.

My head breaks the surface and I take huge gulps of air, spitting as the muddy water trickles down into my mouth.

There's no laughter any more, just the steady thumping of blood in my ears.

Matt and his mates have gone.

I swim to the edge and pull myself out of the pond. My shoes squelch as I get to my feet. My clothes are filthy, and so soaked that they stick to my body. I spit but I can't get the muddy taste out of my mouth.

I know it's stupid, but I'm not thinking about Matt or Cheesy or Joe. I'm thinking about Stonebird. I wanted him to stop the bullying. I wanted him to protect me from Matt and his mates. He looked after Mum and he looked after Jess, but he's definitely not looking after me now.

'What happened to you?' Jess says, when I get back that afternoon.

'I fell in the pond.'

The only spare clothes at school were in the lost-property bin. I'm wearing rugby shorts that are way too tight and a really baggy blue jumper that almost reaches down to my knees. I look ridiculous.

'You look like you got dressed in a tornado,' she says.

'Thanks.'

As I'm heading up to my room, I notice something on the stairs.

Grandma's diary!

Mum must have put it there this morning. I quickly look around to make sure no one's watching, then pick it up and take it upstairs.

I sit on my bed and open the diary, and Mum was right. There is a missing page.

It's been torn out. You can tell because the edge is all jagged and you can see where words have been ripped in half.

The entry straight after the torn page is much shorter than any of the others I've read:

17 January, 1941

I can't face seeing that church any more.
I'm going to have to find a new way home from school.

That seems pretty weird, considering she loved drawing Stonebird so much. Why would she want to avoid it? Unless . . .

I turn back to the earlier entry:

15 January, 1941

Claire's getting worse.
She tried to chase me into the church today.
She said I'm next. She said it's my turn for the ritual.

The ritual again. Grandma's sounding really scared, and it looks as if it's all because of this Claire girl. Did she catch her? Did she lock Grandma inside the church?

175

I flick back through some of the later entries, but there's nothing to say what happened on 16 January.

Claire . . .

The name sounds familiar, and not just from Grandma's diary. The date does too. I feel as though I've heard it somewhere before. But where?

26

You know it's going to be a bad day when lunch ends like this:

'Oi! Short shorts! Tell us a story!'

Move move move move.

Thumping footsteps behind me. I race across the playground, not wanting to turn around because then I'll know how close they are. Better not to know. Better to try to ignore them and focus on my legs moving quicker and quicker.

Over the hopscotch and the tree game no one understands, past the shed . . .

Just keep moving.

'What's wrong?' one of them shouts.

'Tell us about the gargoyle, Liam!'

'Can it do my gardening?'

The footsteps are louder now – they're right behind me. I'm running, not even thinking, just running. Round the corner and through the doors and –

I crash straight into Mrs Culpepper, scattering books everywhere.

'Oh!' she squeals.

Now I glance back.

There they are, through the door. All three of them, with Matt in front. But they're not coming in. They've stopped on the other side. Slowly they turn around, swaggering and spitting, and walk off.

'No, no, don't worry about those!' says Mrs Culpepper, when I crouch to help her with the books. 'Actually you're just the person I was looking for. The headmistress would like to see you. It's important.'

'Right . . .'

'Are you OK, Liam?' she asks. 'Why were you running?'

'Oh, nothing,' I say. 'Just in a hurry to get to class.'

I guess I should start again. You know it's going to be a bad afternoon when you get chased into school and crash into your teacher and find out that the headmistress wants to see you.

I knock on her door three times and stand back,

waiting. The hall is lined with photos of all the different classes in the school, alongside pictures drawn and painted by kids. The smell of coffee wafts from the staffroom a few doors down. Through the window I can see the Year One boys and girls being walked back into the building by their teacher.

Chatting chatting chatting. They're talking and smiling and looking so happy.

Mrs Willis pokes her head out of the door and says, 'You can come in now, Liam.'

I can hear my heart. *Thump thump thump thump.* Even though I can't think of anything I've done wrong. *The headmistress!* It's like when you walk past a policeman and it feels as if they're watching you and even though you haven't done anything it makes you think *What if I have?*

Jess says that if you break the rules at her school, you get detention. We don't have detention here, but I've seen some people have to stay inside when everyone else gets to go out for lunch, or they have to sit in the corner and not take part in the lesson.

Head down, I follow the headmistress into her study. There's a green leather chair behind a wooden desk, which has photos of her and her family on it.

'No need to look so guilty,' says Mrs Willis. She leans

over the desk and smiles, which makes the three grey hairs on her chin poke in different directions. 'Your mother has called to let us know that your grandmother is in a bad way again. She says she's arranged for you to go to the Higgins' house after school.'

'The Higgins' . . . ?'

Then I get it. Matt's house. Again.

She must see something in my face, because she smiles her whiskery smile.

'It's not that bad,' she says. 'I'm sure it won't be for long.'

Matt smirks when I get back to class, like he already knows the news and has planned how he's going to torture me. He leans back in his chair and stares at me, and I can feel his eyes on my back as I sit down at the desk.

Tell us a story, Liam. It goes round and round in my head.

Tell us a story, Liam.

Tell us a story.

So I do.

Later on, when we're sitting in the circle on the floor and the magic egg is soaking up words and there is quiet in the classroom, quiet except for the stories and the gasps – later on, I tell a story about Stonebird and Matt.

I thought it would be hard but it's not.

When the egg gets to me, I close my eyes.

I remember them running after me, remember the pond water rushing up my nose. I picture their faces and hear the sound of their voices.

Even remembering makes my heart beat faster. The egg's warm in my hands and the words spring to my mouth. They flow easily, like they've always been there, like they're waiting to be spoken out loud.

The gargoyle smelt something on the air, I say.

In the cold and the dark, sitting on the roof of its haunted church, it raised its great stone nose and sniffed. And what it smelt was boys. Stupid boys out too late, out in the lane below.

I look up. They're all staring at me, the whole class, because I'm the one with the egg. But Matt and his mates? They're not like the others. They know what I'm talking about, because what I'm talking about is them.

They know it.

I can see in their eyes that they know it.

Stonebird didn't protect me before, so I've got to make sure he protects me now.

The gargoyle sees them, I say. *Sees the lads, swaggering about like they own the place. But the gargoyle is as old as the stones and the wind and the trees. The gargoyle has been in this village for longer than any kid, and it doesn't like people swaggering on its land.*

It watches, from the rooftop.

Waiting.

And when the kids get too close, the gargoyle jumps, down down down, gliding on the wind under the stars. The gargoyle's massive and its wings are heavier than cars, but when it flies it's like a bird.

The kids, there's three of them, and they see something now.

A shadow, passing over the road.

They look at each other and their eyes are wide and they don't know what to do.

One of them says, 'Who's there?'

But there's no answer. The gargoyle can listen and understand and know, but it can't speak. Its language is the language of eyes and beak and claws.

'We're not scared!' says the biggest kid.

And that's when the gargoyle thuds down on to the road, crouching low, glaring. Its eyes are made of moonlight and its tail swipes back and forth. The boys take a step back, and another, and they turn to run –

But the gargoyle is faster. It chases them, beating its

stone wings, chases them and catches the leader of them and the kid screams, but his friends just run. They don't even look back.

The boy cries out and cries out but there's no one left to hear him.

No one to see him get carried off, into the night.

27

The class is so quiet you could hear a bug scurrying along the windowsill.

I hold the egg out for the next person in the circle, but they don't take it. It's only then that I look around and see their faces. All of them, mouths open. Once when I was a little kid I was playing with Jess in her room and I saw one of those French Fries crisps on the floor. I flicked it, just flicked it like you'd flick a greenfly on your clothes, and it shot through the air and straight into her mouth. I'm not even kidding, it got stuck in there, poking out as if she was trying to smoke it.

Even if I tried a million times I'd never be able to do that again.

Except if I tried it now, with my class.

Because their mouths are open caves.

I look from face to face. I'm still holding out the egg, but no one's taking it. Matt's lips are so tight they're just one long thin line across the bottom of his pale face. He's gripping his knees and rocking back and forth. His mates nod at each other and stare back at me and there's a message in their eyes and the message is this: YOU'RE DEAD.

Mrs Culpepper stands up and takes the egg. 'I think that's enough storytelling for one day,' she says.

She puts the egg in the drawer and slams it shut. There's a look on her face that I've never seen before.

When the bell goes at the end of school, I don't get up. I don't leave. I just wait, wait for everyone to push their chairs under their desks and get their bags and their coats from the pegs outside. Wait for them to go.

Matt and his friends are first out the door as soon as the clock hits quarter past three. But they'll be waiting for me. I know it.

I sit until I'm the last one in the room. Just me and Mrs Culpepper. She looks up from her desk and is about to say something when a woman pokes her head in and says, 'Is this Mrs Forrester's class?'

'No,' says Mrs Culpepper. She glances at me again.

I've never seen her look so disappointed. But when she stands up, all she says is, 'Here, I'll show you.'

And then it's just me. I grab my bag and walk to the door. Peeking through the glass I can see the corridor outside. Empty. That's how it seems, anyway. They could be anywhere. But they'll probably wait in the courtyard between the school and the playground where the parents are, because there's a flint wall there blocking them from view.

The door handle feels cold after the warmth of the egg.

Once I'm out of the classroom I turn left, away from the exit, through another door towards the toilets.

If I can just hide in here for a few minutes, then . . .

Then what?

They're bound to look for me. They'll probably find me even in the loos. It's not like there are many places to hide in school, and if I don't go past them, they'll know I'm inside somewhere.

The toilet smells of soap and stale wee. I can feel my shoes sticking to the floor as I walk to the nearest cubicle and lock the door behind me. Whenever someone hides in a loo on TV the baddie always checks under the door, so I put the lid down and sit on it and lift my feet up.

Just a few minutes . . .

I glance at my watch and follow the second hand as it tick-tick-ticks around.

Quarter past becomes half past becomes four o'clock and there's still no sign of them. But I can't bring myself to move. I don't even dare breathe. Not properly. Not freely, in case they're outside, listening, waiting for me to slip up.

I keep telling myself *just a few minutes, just a few minutes*, but the minutes tick by until I've been there for an hour. The lights only go on if there's movement, so I'm sitting in darkness now. I picture the school being locked up and here's me just trapped inside, with no way out and nothing to eat or drink, just waiting until some cleaner discovers me in the morning. But it's OK – it's music club this evening. The school won't get locked until six.

After a while I have to cover my nose from the smell. Darkness and soap and wee, thick in the air. There's only one small window, over by the sink, and the sun's moved on so it's just this weak grey light getting darker and darker.

To keep from getting bored I try to remember things about Grandma. I know Mum dropped Jess and me off at Grandma and Granddad's house once when she went to a wedding in Bath. But all I can remember is feeling annoyed about it. Before you go somewhere you don't want to go, you always make out in your head that it's going to be pointless and annoying. But then it's never really as bad as you expect.

Grandma took us to the pub. I remember now. She took us to the pub in the village and there was a Shakespeare play on in the garden. It was loud and confusing and it went on for practically a hundred years, and I couldn't really understand what was going on. But Grandma and Granddad loved it, so I pretended to enjoy it too, because they were really trying to give us a good time.

They can't have a good time any more.

Granddad is dead and Grandma has got a demon in her head making her forget everything.

I wish Matt and his friends would forget me.

Just this once.

Just now, so I can go home.

But they don't.

CRASH! The outside door swings open. Footsteps on the sticky floor. Quiet voices. I try to breathe as quietly as I can. The bathroom light flickers on and I can see shadows moving under the door. My heart drums louder than their voices, so loud that I know they'll hear it.

The toilet door's locked, but could they break through? I'm fast, but there are three of them, and I'll never get out before they grab me.

I don't usually pray very much but I'm praying now, praying to God and Jesus and Zeus and King Arthur and Robin Hood and praying to Nancy Wake the White Mouse, just praying praying praying that they don't hurt me.

'Oh, Liam!' Matt calls, in a horrible baby voice.

'Come out, Liam!'

'We won't hurt you. We just want to give you a little wash.'

Giggling. Another crash as they kick open the end cubicle.

There are only three cubicles. They'll kick my door next and find it's locked and know I'm in here and there's no way, no way I'll be able to get away. I keep picturing the rush of water on my face when they shove my head into the bog and trying to breathe but finding no air, no air, no air.

I need to get out of here . . .

BANG! They kick on the door.

BANG!

'Liam, we know you're in there!'

Rattle-rattle-rattle-rattle. I check the hinges, but they're thick and metal and not moving. There's no way they can break through. Surely.

BANG!

'Open the door!'

I don't say a thing. Don't move my mouth, even though there's nothing to lose any more. Then I get an idea. I have to do something. So what I do is this.

I crouch on the lid of the toilet. I reach out my right hand, slowly, slowly and as quietly as I can, until my fingers touch the cold metal of the lock.

And then I unlock the door.

Bit by bit.

Clenching my teeth, straining so hard not to make a noise, easing the lock open.

Every now and then I stop and listen.

Every now and then they kick the door with another BANG and it rattles on its hinges and I draw back, chewing my lips. But every time it goes quiet again I tug lightly on the lock.

Slowly slowly slowly slowly . . .

One more centimetre and it's open.

One last little bit.

They kick on the door again and this time it swings in. I ram it with my shoulder and it smacks Matt in the face and he falls back into the sink. The other two don't even know what's going on. Without looking, without even thinking, I run.

28

When I was five I used to want those trainers with red flashing lights on the soles.

I thought they would make me run faster because they look Amazing with a capital A. I know they don't actually make you run faster. I know that now. But even so I still wish I had them. Anything, anything to help me get away.

'It's him!'

'Grab him!'

A door slams and there are footsteps behind me, pounding, chasing, hunting. Across the hall and out the door I go, up the stairs over the bank and into the big playground.

The gate is so far away.

I don't stop for a second – just charge on.

It's dark now, and I can see my breath puffing in the air. Every breath stings my lungs. My ears are burning. I try to rub the sweat from my eyes, but it makes them water more. Ahead of me, an orange glow from the street lights flows over the gate, painting it golden.

I can get there. I know I can get there.

I leap over the gate and run up School Street, towards my lane. Towards home.

No –

Not home. I wasn't even thinking about it, but now I know it's true.

The church. I need to get to the church.

I glance over my shoulder. They're closing in, faces set in anger. They look like gargoyles themselves, or demons.

Come on, Liam . . . run!

But as I turn back my foot catches, the toe of my shoe scrapes on the road, and the tarmac rises up to smack my face.

Black. All I can see is black. Black and grey flecks. I can't see a thing, can't hear anything apart from my own heart. Apart from the blood in my ears.

No. That's not right.

Because if I can hear that, then I should be able to hear their footsteps.

Unless they've stopped.

Unless they've . . .

'Hello, Liam.'

It's Matt's voice. I blink and rub my eyes, trying to clear them, but it doesn't work.

Someone grabs my shirt and hauls me up. I try to find my footing but I can't get a proper grip on the floor. My legs feel stringy and weak. They buckle beneath me, but hands on my collar hold me up.

'We've been waiting for you for a long time,' says Matt, flecks of spit hitting my face. 'We wanted to have words, didn't we, lads? We wanted to have a *little chat.*'

'I didn't mean it,' I say. My voice sounds as if it's coming from someone else. 'It was just a story. It didn't mean anything.'

Laughter rings in the cold and the dark.

'Did you hear that?' says Matt. '"Just a story," he says. This is just a story too.'

I'm falling before the pain hits.

I crash on to the road and hear someone groan – was it me? – and then there's just burning, the burn in my stomach where he punched me.

'Nowhere to run now, little Liam,' says Joe. He sounds close. He's probably standing right over me. 'Nowhere for you to escape. No –' He stops suddenly.

I look up out of instinct, but still all I can see is darkness.

There are no hands holding me now. I shuffle back. Their voices have gone so quiet they're just frightened whispers. Shivers race up and down my neck.

A retching scream rips through the air and at first I think it's one of them, but it can't be, because it's high, high in the sky. Cold air blasts me from above and I can hear the *thump thump thump* of heavy wings.

The next scream definitely *is* one of them.

The others soon join in. Screams and shouts and wails.

Someone cries, 'Run!' and the footsteps pound louder than ever as they tear away from me. I rub my eyes, desperate to see. I need to see this moment, need to see Stonebird, because it *is* him, I know it.

When my sight finally returns I just sit there in the road, blinking. There's blood on my knees where I fell. My hands are throbbing and scratched. I lie back for a second. I'll get up in a minute, but it hurts, everything hurts so much.

That's when I see it.

There's something in the road. No, not something. Some*one*. *Matt!*

His body's so still. Just a dark lump in the middle

of the road, and all of a sudden I've forgotten how to breathe. I glance around, up and down the road, but we're all alone.

What if I've killed him?

Pain rips up the side of my body as I rush over to him. I crouch down and look at his face. There's a swollen red lump on his forehead, oozing blood. Quickly I put my fingers up to his neck, like I've always seen on TV.

Please don't be dead . . .

His pulse beats gently against my fingers.

He's alive.

He's alive!

But what am I going to do? Did the others see what happened? No, it was their scream tearing at the air, their footsteps pounding away into the night. They must have left before this happened. My heart's thumping in my chest and the air's stinging my throat and a thick fog fills my head and I can't think, can't think . . .

They're going to kill me.

Mum.

Gary.

The police.

I'm going to be arrested. I'm going to go to jail.

I could run. I could run like Matt's friends did, leave

him here, get away. No one's seen me. No one knows. I could run home and explain it all away and –

A smear of Matt's blood on my hand clears my head. Rivers of red are trickling down the side of his face. And that's when I know I can't run. I can't. Cheesy and Joe left him, but I won't.

He must have his phone on him. I dig inside his coat pocket, and there it is. Three missed calls flash up from his dad, but it's not him I need to ring. Not yet.

OK. Come on, Liam. Breathe.

I've never called 999 before, but I know what to do. I jab the buttons on the phone. My chest feels heavy and the cold air stings my throat. The phone rings twice and then a woman's voice answers.

'Emergency – what service do you require?'

Matt's eyelids flicker. The blood's dripping off his cheek and on to the road. The words are on my lips but they don't come out.

'Hello?'

'Um, ambulance, please.'

'I'm connecting you now. Please stay on the line.'

'Come quickly, he's – there's a lot of blood.'

'OK, I need you to stay calm and tell me where you are.'

'We're in the road. He's lying in the road.'

'I need an address.'

'Swanbury. School Street in Swanbury.'

'Stay calm. Is anyone else with you?'

'No, it's just me and Matt.'

'What's your name?'

'Liam.'

'Listen to me, Liam. Where's the blood coming from?'

'His head. It's all down his face and on the road. You need to come quick.'

'Help is being arranged as we speak. Just stay calm and keep an eye out for the ambulance. It'll be with you soon.'

'OK,' I say. 'OK.'

'Is he breathing?'

'Yeah. Shall I put him in the recovery position?'

'Don't move him. Just stay calm and wait for the ambulance to arrive.'

'But we're in the middle of the road,' I say.

'Stay where you are, Liam. If any cars come, signal them to stop.'

'OK.'

Come on. Please come on.

I scan the road both ways, desperate to see the flashing lights. My throat's dry. I can see my breath clouding in the orange glow of the street lamps.

'Are you still there?' says the woman.

'Yeah. Please hurry up.'

'An ambulance will be with you very shortly. Is Matt still breathing?'

'Yes, I think so. Oh, hang on . . .'

His chest isn't moving.

I reach down and hold a hand under his nose, but no air comes out.

'No!' I say, panic crashing through me. 'No, he's not.'

The voice in my ear turns into a buzz. I can't hear the words. Matt's stopped breathing and he's going to die and it's all my fault . . .

I sit back and rub the sweat from my forehead and that's when I see the lights.

Blue flashes in the distance, brighter than everything else around me.

'I can see the ambulance,' I say, but my voice is dry and cracked.

'It's going to be OK,' says the operator.

'Thank you.' My eyes are suddenly burning. 'Thank you.'

29

One paramedic puts a yellow jacket over me and moves me out of the road, while the other kneels over Matt.

I try and hear what he's saying, but my mind's too foggy to make out the words.

It's going to be OK, I tell myself.

He's going to be all right.

They slide a stretcher under Matt's back and secure him with straps.

That's when my hand vibrates and I almost drop Matt's phone in shock. It's his dad calling. I hesitate for a second, wanting to ignore it. But I can't. There's no ignoring this. I take a deep breath and answer.

'Where are you?' says the voice on the other end of the line. 'I thought you'd be—'

'It's not Matt, it's Liam,' I say, trying to keep my

voice steady. 'There's – there's been an accident. We're on School Street.'

'What? What happened? Did you call an ambulance?'

'Yeah, they're here now.'

Matt groans, and his eyes flicker open for a second then drift closed.

'I think he's OK,' I say.

'I'm on my way.'

Soon bright headlights appear from the end of the road. The car pulls to a stop and Matt's dad leaps out and rushes over.

'What happened?' he says. He crouches down and strokes Matt's face. 'My God, what happened?'

I try to speak, but my throat clenches and the words don't come out. But Gary doesn't ask me again. He just peers at Matt and whispers, *My son*, over and over. *My son, my son . . .*

Then Matt moves. His eyes blink open and he takes a shuddering breath.

'Dad,' he says, in this thick slurred voice.

'Who did this to you?' says Gary. 'What happened?'

Matt's bleary eyes move from his dad to me, still crouching beside him. *This is it*, I think. I'm going to jail. Matt's mouth moves, trying to form words, and my stomach shrinks and I'm ready to run and –

'Car,' says Matt.

WHAT?

'What?' says his dad.

'A car,' says Matt. 'Came out of nowhere. Knocked me into the wall, and – drove off. Disappeared round the bend.'

I'm looking into Matt's eyes. They're locked on to mine, not moving, not even blinking, and I can see he knows he's lying.

'Are you sure?' says Gary. He frowns, looks at me. 'Liam, did you see it too?'

'I – I don't know,' I say. 'I just found him like this.'

I know it's not the truth, but it's not really a lie either.

'I'm so glad you were here,' Gary says as the paramedics shut the ambulance doors.

I try not to meet his eyes. 'Me too.'

'I'll talk to the paramedics,' he says. 'They'll probably have to phone the police. They'll want to see Matt, I'm sure. They might want to talk to you too.' He looks at his watch, then adds, 'Are you OK getting home? You've got a key?'

'I'm fine,' I say. 'It's only up the road.'

I hand him Matt's phone and walk away quickly. I'm shivering now. I didn't realize how cold it was. I shove

201

my hands in my pockets to try to warm them up. *The police!* What am I going to do?

The moon's low and white and I can see my breath clouding in its light.

A sudden movement makes me stop.

A dark shape flying across the hugeness of the sky, in the direction of the church.

I shouldn't go. I know I shouldn't go. What I *should* do is go home. But I can't bring myself to go back yet. I need to see Stonebird with my own eyes. I need to know for sure that it happened.

My head throbs as I stumble towards the church.

Every time I blink I see Matt's unconscious, blood-smeared face.

What have I done?

The road is quiet. Light from the houses and the street lamps and the moon makes the lane look grey-blue; makes it look like another world.

You're such an idiot, Liam . . .

Telling stupid stories!

Outside the church, the graveyard is thick with shadows.

I try not to think about what's under my feet as I wind my way between the headstones. I don't normally get scared of the dark, but it's hard not to here.

By the old wooden door I stop and listen. I'm scared to go in because if it's true, if it was Stonebird that did it, then what does that make me?

After what feels like a million hours I have to open the door.

Inside, the church is quiet and still. Starlight lightly touches the pews and the pillars, but it's so dark I have to feel my way to the entrance of the crypt. Images flash in my mind and I try to shut them out but I can't. They just stick there. Blood and broken bones and huge terrified eyes.

My neck tingles. There's a crash behind me. I glance back, but there's nothing there.

I turn round again, and that's when I scream.

'No,' I say. 'No . . . no . . .'

Desperately, frantically I scramble back.

Because he's suddenly there.

He's not moving, but he's there, right in front of me.

As big as a tree, rearing up, bright eyes flickering. I need to run.

But I've just seen something else and my legs are limp and all I can do is stand there.

Stonebird's massive clawed hands. They're red.

Matt's blood.

It can't be anything else.

'No,' I say again, but it comes out quiet, just a whimper that vanishes in the dark.

Stonebird's still not moving, but how did he get there how did he get there *how did he get there*?

There was no noise, no nothing, and I was right here the whole time.

'I didn't mean for you to hurt him. I just wanted you to look after me.'

Even if Matt is a bully, he still doesn't deserve what he got tonight. Quickly I get to my feet and I race back down the aisle, not daring to take my eyes off the stone monster, because that's what he is, he's a monster. He's got a kid's blood on his hands.

And it's all my fault.

30

There are no lights on.

That's the first thing I notice.

What time is it? My watch is broken. It must have smashed when I fell. But the night is dark and pinpricked with stars. Even Jess's room is pitch black.

Mum's going to kill me . . .

Every few seconds I glance over my shoulder, expecting to see Stonebird. I didn't hear him in the church, so I doubt I'll hear him if he comes after me now. But there's nothing there.

I sneak across the drive, moving slowly so the gravel doesn't crunch beneath my feet. Then I'm on to the big stone step by the front door.

One more quick glance over my shoulder. Still not there.

Maybe he's stopped chasing me. Maybe he was *never* chasing me. But the way he appeared out of nowhere . . . his hands, the blood, the gleam in his eye . . .

I grab my keys, squinting in the dark and jabbing at the door until they fit into the keyhole. The lock clicks as I turn it. The door creaks open, and the whole time I'm thinking, *Pants pants pants* because it's so loud, everything's so loud. I'm just wondering why everything has to be at its loudest when you're trying to be at your quietest when I tread on Mum's foot and she lets out a yell loud enough to be heard in France.

'Wha—?! *Liam!*' she hisses, jumping up from the chair she was asleep in. 'What are you *doing*? Where have you *been*?'

One more glance back as I close the door. I can't help it.

Nothing.

'I was just—'

'You had me so worried!' Mum says. She grabs my hands and pulls me into a hug. All around her there's a strong smell of wine and I wonder if she's been crying, but I can't see, because she's squeezing me tight and my face is pressed right up against her cardigan. 'I heard about Matt. When you didn't come home I went out looking for you but I couldn't find you and – oh, Liam.'

She holds me for a minute, then pulls away and leads me through to the living room. Daisy's asleep on the sofa, legs stretched out as if she owns the place. Every now and then she twitches and yips and yaps.

A sudden twinge of pain in my jaw makes me wince, and I clear my throat to try to cover it up.

'Are you hurt?' Mum says.

'No, I'm OK, Mum.'

'Please talk to me,' she says, sitting down on the sofa. I slump down next to her. 'What happened? Why are you back so late? Gary said you were coming straight home. Are you . . . ? Are you avoiding me?'

'What? Why would I be avoiding you?'

'Well,' she says. 'Because of Grandma, maybe? I know it's hard, seeing her like she is. God knows I understand. But I need you to know you can talk to me.'

'No, Mum, it's nothing to do with Grandma.'

It's a little bit of a lie, but I can't exactly tell her the truth.

The truth is I told a story with Mrs Culpepper's egg and Stonebird came to life and acted out my words and attacked Matt and put him in hospital. And now he's got blood on his hands. And – and – if Stonebird's got blood on his hands, then I've got blood on my hands too.

There's no difference between me and him.

It's got to stop. No more stories. No more Stonebird.

'What?' says Mum. 'What is it? You're frowning.'

'It's all right, Mum. I just needed a walk. It's all right. I'm sorry for not telling you where I was.'

She doesn't believe me. I can see it in her eyes as they fill up. Her lip trembles and silently the tears trickle down her cheeks, so I hug her close, and she hugs me back, and for a while we just sit there hugging. Not saying a word. Just hugging.

And in her dreams, Daisy wags her tail, *thump thump thump thump*.

It's not long before Mum falls asleep again.

'Goodnight,' I whisper.

I'm just about to go upstairs when it hits me.

Claire.

Just like that, it pops into my head.

Why she sounded so familiar. Why 16 January is such an important date.

I saw her grave outside the church when I was chasing Jess with Daisy. I'm sure I did. But there's only one way to be certain.

Glancing over quickly to make sure Mum's still asleep, I sneak back out of the front door. I close it as quietly as possible, then jog up the lane and slip into the church grounds.

The dark is thick around me now. *There's nothing to worry about*, I tell myself, but every time a shadow moves I flinch.

It's hard to read the tombstones, but I can just about make out the names.

Ryan Brooks.

Sophie Reynolds.

And there –

CLAIRE SMITH
TAKEN TOO YOUNG
12 SEPTEMBER, 1928 – 16 JANUARY, 1941.

Reading it again makes my stomach clench. All this time I've thought the church was safe, but that's not true. Because Claire Smith died on the day of the missing entry: 16 January.

Right around the time she was bullying Grandma.

31

Matt isn't at school the next day.

I sit down at my desk and glance at his, but it's empty.

Cheesy and Joe scowl at me from the back of the class.

'Oi!' they hiss. 'We heard what happened.'

I look round, but Mrs Culpepper's busy wiping the board clean. Everyone else pretends to be working, but I know they're listening in. *They know about Stonebird . . .* News in school travels faster than fish when you tap on their tank. There's no such thing as a secret. If Cheesy and Joe know the truth, then soon the whole class will. I open my notebook and start scribbling to take my mind off them, but then I see the list again. At the bottom, it says, *Stop Matt once and for all.* I didn't mean the words in a bad way, but reading them now makes me feel sick.

'It's your fault he got hit by that car,' says Cheesy.

Car?

I was right. They must have run before Stonebird got there.

I can feel their eyes on the back of my neck. Part of me wants to shrink down and hide under the desk, even though I know they'll just get worse if I do. But I've got to say something, or it'll never stop.

'You're dead,' says Joe.

'No,' I whisper.

'What?'

'No,' I say, turning back to face them. 'It's not my fault. It's your fault, for being scared of a stupid story. You ran off. You're the ones who left him.'

Their eyes bulge in their red faces, but I'm more surprised than they are. I can't believe I just said that. The words just came out, but now I don't know what to say so I turn away quickly. They might not see that I'm shaking.

'You what?' says Joe, scraping his chair back and bolting up.

Mrs Culpepper turns round at the noise. 'What was that?'

'Nothing,' he says. He sits back down, breathing heavily.

Cheesy and Joe can't say anything to that. There's nothing *to* say, because it's true. Yeah, it was my fault Matt got attacked by Stonebird – but they think he got hit by a car. And if we're living this weird lie, then they're as guilty as I am.

Mrs Culpepper writes the timetable on the board, and what it says is this:

9.30 – Maths

10.30 – English

11.30 – Geography

1.30 – Music

2.30 – History

'Miss?' says a girl at the front of the class.

'Yes, Himali, what is it?'

'There isn't any time for the magic egg.'

'No, you're quite right,' says Mrs Culpepper.

'Aren't we going to be telling stories?'

'Not today. We're going to have a break from stories for a while.'

Everyone groans. No more stories. I look away, thankful that they don't know the truth. Mrs Culpepper glances at me, then turns back to the board.

The rest of the class might not know, but she does.

She must do.

32

After school we go to visit Grandma.

Her eyes flutter open when the nurse introduces us, then quickly close.

'She's very tired at the moment,' Mum says.

Jess hugs Mum from the side as I walk up to Grandma's bed and look down at her. Her light blue nightgown looks massive on her. It's baggy all over. Her wrinkly white arms poke out like bones.

'Hi, Grandma,' I say, but she doesn't stir.

Her breath is so quiet.

The other day when Grandma said, *I've killed before*, it was easy to pretend it was just the demon in her. But Claire Smith died on 16 January and Grandma ripped out her diary entry from that day, and why would you do that if you didn't have something to do with it?

I realize I'm frowning at her, and try to cover it up by looking round the room.

On the bedside cabinet there are three photos. The first one is Grandma and Granddad on a holiday in Hawaii. They've got pink and yellow flower necklaces around their shoulders and these big, big smiles that mean they're Truly Happy. You don't see smiles that big very often. People on TV smile in shows and movies, but you can't see the happiness behind their eyes. I've seen about a million photos in my life and there are only a few with smiles like this.

The second photo is of Mum. She's holding a baby in her arms, and her face is chalky and there are bags under her eyes, but you can see she's happy too. The baby is me.

And the third photo is Jess. She's grinning the kind of grin where her teeth stick right out like a monkey's.

Three photos and all of them are so happy, in a room that's quiet and colourless and nearly empty except for my tiny Grandma.

'It's OK,' says Mum, behind me. 'We can come back later.'

But I don't move. I need to know. I need to find out if she really did kill Claire.

Grandma turns over in bed and looks up at me. It's funny how the only things that don't get old and wrinkly are a person's eyes. They're so shiny. Brand-new, almost. Bright and marble-like, as blue as summer. But there's something in them that lets you know they're old. Or not old exactly. Just that they've seen a lot of things.

'How are you, dear?' Grandma's voice creaks when she speaks, making every word sound as though it needs a walking stick.

'I'm OK,' I lie.

'You look a hundred miles away,' she says, and chuckles to herself. Every word comes out of her mouth so slowly, but her eyes are bright. 'My mother used to say that about me, you know. We would walk to the beach up in Whitley Bay, and on a summer's day the sea would lap at the shore and I would look out at it. Watching the mist rising. Watching the never-ending blue.'

I look at Mum, heart racing. Jess is surprised too, I can see it. *Maybe Grandma's getting better.* Mum just smiles sadly at me, as if she can read my mind but doesn't want to let me down. She shakes her head and turns back to the bed.

I follow her eyes. Grandma's chewing at the top of her nightgown, gnawing it with her back teeth. A second is all it takes and she's completely different, a whole other person.

'Oh, hello, dear,' she says when she sees me watching, as though it's in no way weird to chew your clothes. 'You look a hundred miles away.'

She stops chewing, lies back and chuckles to herself.

'Do you know,' Grandma says, 'my mother used to say that to me, when I was a young lady. *You look a hundred miles away*, she'd say.'

I step back from the bed. I can't ask her. Not now. Not like this.

A hand touches my shoulder. It's Mum, with that sad smile still on her face.

'Hi,' Mum says to Grandma, and I can hear the strain as she tries to sound happy. 'It's us. It's Sue and Jess and Liam.'

Grandma jolts back, frowns slightly, all the blankness gone. Her eyes move from face to face, and then it hits, and she smiles again, although it almost looks like a grimace.

'Oh, how lovely!' she says.

For the rest of the visit, she drifts in and out of sleep. When she talks, she says random fragments about nothing, things that don't make sense.

Like, 'Where did it go?'

Like, 'I did look after them, didn't I?'

Like, 'What are we doing, Arthur?'

And when you ask her what she means, she's already forgotten what she said.

When Grandma falls asleep for the fourth time, Mum taps me on the shoulder and says it's time to leave. I'm last out of the room, because I stay there looking at her for a minute, just trying to work it out.

Where does the demon come from? How does it choose what to eat? And how can Grandma remember some things from her life so clearly, but recent stuff is there one second and gone the next? Like someone flashing past on the train. You see them and they might notice you and you wonder about them for a second, but then they're whizzing off and a few moments later they're gone from your life.

Walking back down the corridor to the exit, I spot something that makes me stop.

The name on the plaque beside one of the doors says Isabelle Higgins.

Mum and Jess are further up the corridor. Soon they'll be at the door and going out to the car. But the name tugs at something in my mind.

The door's half open. Through the crack I can see into a room laid out just like Grandma's. Even the window's the same, but this one doesn't look over the garden. The view is of the edge of the car park leading on to the street.

In the bed there's a woman. She's not like the others in the care home. She's younger. She's got long blonde hair and her skin has real colour to it and no wrinkles. Her nails are painted red. The room is bursting with colour from flowers and paintings and the TV. It's alive.

But the woman's just lying there. I can see her eyes are open, but she's just staring at the ceiling, not doing anything much at all. And –

No, it can't be.

The picture in Matt's house. This woman looks just like her. A bit older maybe, but not much.

I inch closer. She's talking to herself. Whispering things.

I hold my ear to the gap between the door and the wall. It feels like my heart's in my throat. I shouldn't be here. I shouldn't be seeing this.

'Liam!' calls Jess from down the hall.

They're waiting there, both of them, standing in the doorway.

It comes to me when we're in the car on the way home. *Higgins.*

It's Matt's surname.

33

Over a week passes before Matt comes back to school.

He just walks in halfway through the day, in the middle of a lesson on the War. The board's covered in all these amazing drawings and Mrs Culpepper has labelled all the planes.

Everyone turns to see him standing in the doorway. His arm is in plaster and in a sling. I hold my breath, waiting for him to say something, but he doesn't, just strolls over to his desk and sits in silence.

'Welcome back, Matt,' says Mrs Culpepper. 'I'm glad you're OK.'

After lunch Mrs Culpepper says we can pass the magic egg round. She looks at me as she says it, and I can see the warning in her eyes.

The class practically explodes when she takes the

egg out. They leap up and shove their chairs under the table and rush to sit in a circle before she's even said anything.

I'm the last to sit down. There's no way I can tell a story about Stonebird again. I promised myself I would stop. But all I've ever done when I've held that egg is make up stories about him. What else can I say?

Mrs Culpepper sits on the floor cross-legged with the rest of us, but she doesn't pass the egg on like normal. She cups it in front of her, holding it right up before her eyes. She waits for everyone to settle down and get quiet before she speaks.

'I thought I'd join in today,' she says. 'It's been a while since I've told a story.'

Her eyes move around the circle. They linger longest on me.

'I'm going to tell you a secret,' she says. 'When your headmistress interviewed me for this job, she asked me what my weakness was. It's a tricky question, isn't it? Having to admit you're bad at something. But for me it's easy. My weakness is my mother. I love her very much. I'd do anything for her.'

She moves the egg around in her hands, rubbing it with her thumb.

Then she looks up. She's *staring* at me.

'Mrs Willis also asked me why I wanted to work here, so far from my home in Scotland. "I go where I'm needed," I said. I hope you think I've helped, even if in some cases I haven't quite helped enough.'

Why won't she stop looking at me? I pretend to fiddle with the sleeve of my jumper, and when I look up again she's squinting at the little blue veins in the egg.

'Soon I might have to go back,' she says. 'My mother – she's not very well. The doctors thought she might get better, but it seems they were wrong.'

Hands shoot into the air. There's an explosion of voices.

'But, miss!'

'You can't go!'

'You're the best teacher in the whole school!'

But Mrs Culpepper just holds up the egg. She taps it with her finger, reminding us of Rule Number One: only the person with the egg can talk, and the class falls silent. She smiles a sad smile.

'Thank you,' says Mrs Culpepper. 'Who knows – maybe I won't have to. But I'm just letting you know that I might. And if do, I'll be taking this,' she says, holding up the egg, staring at me over the top of it. 'So make use of it while you can.'

And all I can think is – *What?*

Why is she looking at me like that? Make use of it how? What am I supposed to say?

She passes the egg, and the class tell stories about their favourite aeroplanes and what they dreamed about last night, and all of it's linked, all of it comes back to Mrs Culpepper and what we've learned in her lessons.

Then it's my turn and the egg is thrust into my hand, and even though I can feel its warmth seeping into me, my tongue is dry and my voice has run away.

I've always loved stories. My head's normally filled with characters and weird names. But not now. Now it's only filled with ringing silence.

I sit there for a minute, the egg in my hand, but nothing comes.

'Liam, are you OK?' says Mrs Culpepper.

'Yes,' I say, without looking up.

My palms are hot and sweaty. The egg's heavy in my hands. I can feel a million eyes burning into me but I try to ignore them.

Come on, say something, anything . . .

My knuckles are white. My hands are shaking. I want to tell a story to make everything OK but I don't know how.

There's nothing to say.

Nothing that can make any of it better.

Grandma's rotting away, probably dying, and I attacked Matt and put him in hospital and just thinking about it makes hundreds of eels slip and slide in my stomach, and what good are words now?

The egg falls out of my hands and rolls across the carpet.

The stories made me feel like a superhero, like I could make a difference. With Stonebird as my friend, I thought I could do anything. But I can't think of him any more. I have to cut him out, because it's too easy to make a mistake, to get carried away.

And without him, I'm empty.

Without him, I'm useless.

When I get home, I go straight to my room.

Everything's so loud in my head.

Mrs Culpepper might be leaving. I've never had a teacher like her before. She's kind and easy to talk to and she can make the most boring stuff seem really interesting because she gets so excited about it. If she leaves, who's going to do the story circle?

She can't leave. I need her.

And Grandma . . . I'm so sure that she killed Claire. But who am I to say anything? I could have done the same to Matt.

Mrs Culpepper tried to warn me. She said gargoyles can be dangerous.

But I thought I could control him. I thought I could get him to do what I wanted, but I can't. Once the words leave my mouth, they're not mine any more. They belong to Stonebird. And he can do what he wants with them.

Claire Smith. Taken too young.

The diary's still on my bedroom floor, but I don't look at it. Instead I grab my phone. Now I know her surname, I search for *Claire Smith Swanbury 1941*. I can't believe it's taken me so long to do this.

A story comes up on the website for the *Swanbury Reporter*. It's a scan of an old newspaper clipping, with an ancient-looking font and a weird logo:

CHURCH CATASTROPHE – TERROR AS ROOF CAVES IN

A Swanbury family has been left devastated after the roof of the local church collapsed on their 13-year-old daughter –

The church!

So that's why it's such a wreck.

And if it happened in the church, then –

Stonebird. It has to be. Grandma must have used Stonebird to kill her.

34

In the morning I eat breakfast in silence. I'm trying not to blink because every time I close my eyes I see Grandma standing over the dead body of Claire in the broken church. Mum's emptying the dishwasher and Jess has barely looked up since I entered the room.

'What's going on with you two?' Mum says after a while.

'Nothing,' Jess mumbles.

Mum looks from Jess to me and back. 'That's precisely my point,' she says. She sits down next to us and sighs. 'Look, I know things have been – well, not great recently. But I want you both to know that I love you. Liam, you were so brave last week with Matt. And Jess, your form teacher says your attendance is right up. I'm really proud of you. Both of you.'

I smile a *thank you* at Mum, even though if she knew

the truth she wouldn't be proud of me at all. She's trying to be cheerful, trying to be strong for us. It hasn't been wine o'clock for a week. I cross my fingers and silently wish that she can stay like this, no matter how bad Grandma gets.

Jess doesn't look up though. She's fiddling with her thumbs.

'So, Jess,' Mum says, 'I was wondering . . . how about we invite Ben round for dinner later?'

That puts a smile on Jess's face.

Normally we eat dinner in the living room, but Mum sets out four places at the dining table especially. Earlier on she shut Daisy in the utility room and said we're not allowed to let her out until everyone's finished. Now Daisy's bouncing up and down so she can peer out of the window. Her ears flap like tiny wings every time she disappears out of sight. I think the smell of the food is driving her crazy.

'What's the time?' says Jess, even though there's a clock above the fridge.

'Coming up to six,' I say.

'Oh, where is he?' she says.

Wine o'clock started half an hour ago and Mum's already at Stage Two.

I've worked out that there are four stages, and they go like this:

- One glass = humming
- Two glasses = singing
- Three glasses = mixing up words
- Four glasses = crying

I hope she doesn't go past Stage Three tonight.

There's a knock at the door just as Mum starts frying the chicken, and Jess bolts off the chair to answer it. I hear Ben saying something and Jess saying, *You look fine*, and then they both come into the kitchen. I have to look away to stop from laughing because Ben's dressed in a shirt and tie with a jacket that's so big the sleeves hang over his hands.

'Hello, Mrs Williams,' he says.

'Hello, Ben,' says Mum. She grins and turns away. 'Sit down guys. It'll be ready in a minute.'

'All right, Liam?' says Ben, as he and Jess shuffle into the dining room.

'Hi,' I say.

I pull a face at Jess and she gives me a look that says, *DON'T SAY ANYTHING*, so I don't, because Ben seems nice and I want it to go well for them.

Jess sits next to Ben and leans close to him.

'Have you washed your hair since school?' she whispers.

'Maybe,' he says.

She barges him playfully and looks up at me. 'How was school?' she asks.

'All right,' I say.

In the kitchen, Mum's voice rises above the sound of the sizzling chicken. She's making up a song, humming the tune louder and louder.

'Here you are, kiddos,' she says, bringing the plates over two at a time. She sits next to me and puts down her glass and wine sloshes all over the table. 'Oops,' she says, giggling to herself, and she gets up to fetch some kitchen roll.

'Sorry,' says Jess, under her breath.

Ben shakes his head, as if to say, *Don't worry about it.*

No one speaks when Mum gets back. Jess just looks at her food and Ben looks at Jess and Mum's looking round at all of us with blurry eyes and a big smile on her face. I've seen that smile before, when we visited Grandma in the home for the first time. I asked, *Are you OK?* and Mum said, *Yes*, and she smiled that smile and I said, *Are you sure?* and she said, *Yes*, but then her smile wobbled and tears started running down her cheeks.

Everything she does makes it seem like she's happy. The singing and the humming and calling us *kiddos*. It's like what you'd find in a school textbook if you were learning about *happy*.

But something's not right. It's too happy. And that makes me think that maybe she's not happy at all.

'This looks amazing,' I say, trying to make her happy for real. I start scoffing even though the chicken's so hot it burns the top of my mouth.

'Yeah,' says Ben. 'Great. Really great.'

'That's very kind of you,' Mum says.

There's quiet for a long time. Then Ben looks up and says, 'It must be hard.'

And Mum says, 'What must?'

And Ben says, 'You know – having your mum in a home. It must be hard.'

Jess and I glance at each other and I know we're thinking the same thing.

'It is,' Mum says. 'She's not much of a talker any more . . .'

'My nan's hilarious. She shouts at the TV like it can hear her. You never know what she's going to say next.'

My heart crashes in my chest and I stop eating so I can listen, but all the while I'm thinking, *No no no no –*

Mum's smiling that sad smile again. 'I'd love to be

able to talk to my mum properly. Even just for a moment. Part of me would anyway . . .' She stops and downs the rest of her drink and closes her eyes tight shut. When she opens them again she says, 'But part of me – part of me thinks she would be better off dead.'

The silence rings. Mum looks up as if she's surprised herself. I pull a face that's meant to tell her to change the subject, but it doesn't work.

'Sorry,' she says. 'It's been a bit of a rough day.'

It looks as if she wants to say more, but she stops. Tears well up in the corners of her eyes. She tries to smile around at us, but her lips wobble and now the tears are trickling down her cheeks and falling on the table.

'What is it?' I say. 'Is it Grandma? Is she OK?'

'Not really,' Mum says, her voice cracking. 'She could barely open her eyes today. She's in constant pain. She's thinner than ever. I think – I think we're going to have to get used to the idea that she may not be around for much longer.'

She pours another drink.

Everyone looks away, at the table or the walls or the floor.

The food's still hot but I wolf it down, trying not to meet anyone's eyes.

There's no way this is going to end well.

35

'I need you – to – listen to me,' says Mum, spilling wine over her top as she tries to sit up. 'I want you to – go to . . .' She lurches to her feet, holding the coffee table to steady herself. She reaches out, trying to grab my shoulder, trying to bring me close but stumbling and falling.

'Mum!' I prop her up, help her back to the sofa.

'Liam,' she says. 'I'm so sorry. About all of this.'

Her voice comes in bursts, the words all tumbling over themselves.

There's an empty bottle of wine on the table, and another on the floor by her feet that's half full of dark red liquid. Mum's eyes flutter and close, then burst open again and she reaches up, trying to grab me.

Dark make-up streaks run down her cheeks. There are tissues on the table so I grab one and dab Mum's face. She tries to fight it but settles back, eyes closed, whispering words that don't make sense.

Jess appears at the doorway with Ben beside her, looking in.

'Are you sure she's all right?' says Ben.

'She's fine,' says Jess. She looks at me. 'We're going out for a bit. I'll see you later.'

Then she's gone, leaving me here with Mum practically knocked out on the sofa. The dinner went better than I thought it would. I think Mum even *liked* talking about Grandma, but she finished the bottle of wine she was on and started another and now she's well past Stage Four and probably even at Stage Five, and I've never seen that before.

Daisy trots over to Mum with her tail between her legs. She sniffs Mum's hand, then looks at me and I can see in her eyes that she's worried, so I stroke her head and talk to her until she settles down.

'Liam . . .' says Mum, in this soft moaning voice. She's got her eyes closed. She twitches and groans and moans my name again.

'Mum?' I say, shaking her shoulder. 'Mum, are you OK?'

Nothing. I shake her again. 'Mum!' I say, louder this time. But she's just deadweight slumped on the sofa.

She's not opening her eyes. 'Mum, can you hear me?'

The silence is so heavy I can hear my heart racing. *Why?* Why is this happening? Why are you doing this? Something burns inside me, anger at Jess for leaving me with Mum. How is she so OK with this? *Come ON, Mum!*

Her mouth hangs open as if frozen mid-yawn. She's breathing at least. Her shoulders rise up and down in a slow, steady rhythm. Hands shaking, I lift up one of her eyelids. Her eye is staring straight up, flickering back and forth –

Quickly I jerk my hand away. *Why why why . . . ?*

Mum always leaves her laptop under the coffee table. I grab it and go to Google and type *how to look after really drunk people*, because that's what Mum is. And what it says is this:

- Don't let the intoxicated person fall asleep on their own.
- Stay with them until help arrives.
- If they do fall asleep, make sure you lie them sideways so they don't drown on their own sick.
- Check them regularly to make sure they respond.

Mum's already fallen asleep. But at least I'm here, so she doesn't have to pass out on her own. Rule Number Two means I've got to call for help. In *Superman* he has such good hearing that he could probably hear Mum sleeping and he would know to come over, but Superman isn't real, so I've got to make sure someone else knows about her.

999.

That's the first number that comes to my head. It worked with Matt, but you get in trouble for ringing 999 when it's not an emergency, and I'm not sure this is one. But who else can I ring? The phone's in the corner of the room, and beside it is a little leather notebook of numbers. I flip it open and look through the names inside.

The first one is a person called Auntie Joan, who I've never heard of in my life. If she's an Auntie then maybe she can help, but then I remember that family sometimes live all over the world. Just because she's Auntie Joan doesn't mean she's close Auntie Joan. She could be far-away Auntie Joan.

The second number is someone called Doctor Robert. Doctors are good at helping. Once when I was three I was learning how to ride my bike without stabilizers and I sped down a hill *pedalling pedalling pedalling* but then it got too fast and I couldn't pedal any more and I wobbled off and crashed into a tree. It didn't hurt, not really, but I did have a big cut on my knee, and we had to go to the doctor to get eight stitches.

Maybe I should call this Doctor Robert. But it's past nine o'clock, which means it's late and he might be angry at being disturbed when he's not at work. I remember Dad getting Very Angry when people called him after nine o'clock. He used to swear at them down the phone, a lot. Mum said he swore so much the air would turn blue.

The third name is Gary. Matt's Dad.

Gary is Mum's friend and that means he'll want to help, even if he's angry at me for calling so late. But I haven't seen him since Matt went to hospital. What if he's not just angry because it's late? What if Matt's told him what really happened?

My finger hovers over the phone and it takes ages to press the first number. Then I just press the rest as fast as I can and hold the phone up to my ear. Sometimes you have to get things over with. Like pulling out a tooth that's dangling on the last little bit of gum.

'Hello?' says the voice on the other end.

'Hi, is this Matt's dad?'

'It is, yes. Who am I speaking to?'

'It's Liam. Sue's son.'

'Liam,' he says. 'How can I help?'

'It's Mum. She's drunk and won't wake up and I don't know what to do.'

He says that he'll be around in a minute, and hangs up. I let the phone hum in my ear for a moment before I put it down and turn back to face Mum. She hasn't moved. She's just lying there groaning. Daisy's asleep on the floor in front of her, twitching her paws. Dogs are so happy and free. They don't worry about things that they can't help, like grandmas with demons or horrible kids at school or sisters bunking off school. They just live in the moment. Even if they've had a bad day, you give them food and all of a sudden it's the best day in the history of the world ever.

Sometimes I wish I was a dog.

I sit down next to Mum and hold her hand to let her know I'm there.

Then I remember the list of rules on the Internet, and I poke her arm.

'Mum?'

Nothing.

'Mum?' I say, prodding her again.

She twists and turns and groans. Her eyes flash

open for a moment and she says my name, and I lean in closer saying, *It's OK, it's OK.* It looks like she's about to smile, but then she makes this horrible noise like *HUUUAAAARGH!*

And she throws up all over me.

36

Matt's dad takes longer than a minute, but I'm not surprised, because no one ever means they'll be a minute when they say it.

If you think about it, it's practically impossible to do anything in a minute. Not even Usain Bolt could have got here in a minute from Matt's house.

I've just changed my T-shirt when he knocks on the door.

Daisy scrabbles up and slides on the wooden floor as she runs over to bark at him.

'It's OK, Daisy.' I grab her collar to hold her back.

'Where's your Mum?' says Matt's dad. He's wearing jogging bottoms and a white tank top and has shoes but no socks on.

'In the living room,' I say, pointing back into the hall.

I take him through to where Mum's lying on her side on the sofa.

'I tried to clear up the sick, but . . .'

'Yeah,' he says, grimacing at the smell.

He walks up to Mum and kneels down and brushes the hair out of her face. He grabs a tissue and dabs at her mouth where the sick's still stuck to her. Sometimes when it's really quiet and I don't know what to say, I feel like doing something really crazy just to break the silence. You know, like bust out a really weird dance move or make random noises. Part of me wants to do something like that now, but I don't think Matt's dad will find it very funny. I want him to know I'm not a horrible person. I want him to know I'm sorry for what happened to Matt.

'I searched online for what to do,' I say to his back. 'I made sure she's on her side so she doesn't drown in her sick.'

'You've done well,' he says. 'You seem very good in emergencies.'

'Mr Higgins?'

'Yes?'

My voice catches. 'I'm sorry about what happened to Matt.'

He doesn't say anything to that, just turns back to

Mum, so I kneel down next to Daisy and wait. When Mum opens her eyes again, she jolts up sharply, blinking. She rubs her eyes and her mouth hangs open.

'Gary . . .' she says.

'Shhh. You need to get some rest.'

'Oh, Gary, I'm so sorry,' she mumbles. 'What are you doing here? I didn't call you, did I?'

'No. Liam did.'

Mum looks over at me and her eyes fill with tears again. They overflow and run down the squiggly black tracks left by her make-up. 'My poor boy,' she says, in this whimpering tiny voice. 'Where's Jess?'

'She's gone out.'

'Oh yes, I remember.'

Her voice trails off and she falls back on the sofa. I sit there stroking Daisy, stroking her soft, soft ears. Mum's breathing is heavy and slow.

My heart feels buried deep inside me, and my stomach too. Where they should be is just nothingness, weighing everything down.

Mum's there, but she's not Mum when she's like this.

This must be how Mum feels when she goes to visit Grandma. In my head I keep picturing a world without Mum in it, but it makes my eyes well up, so I just shift closer to Daisy and stroke her to take my mind off it.

Eventually Gary helps Mum upstairs. He rolls her on to her side and sits on the edge of the bed, and I sit next to him, and all around us is dark and silence apart from Mum's breathing, which is slow and steady now.

'It's hard,' he says. He's grimacing. He runs a hand through his hair. 'It's . . .'

He's quiet for ages. The alarm clock beside Mum's bed is one of those really loud ones where you can hear it tick-tocking. Tick. Tock. Tick. Tock. And still Gary doesn't say anything. His eyes flick across to Mum, then back to me and his mouth opens and closes, opens and closes.

'Yeah . . .' I don't know what else to say.

'Listen, Liam. I know what your mum's going through. Probably better than anyone. I'm not sure if you know, but my wife – she's – she's got . . .'

He breaks off and throws up his hands as if to say, *I don't even know what I'm saying.*

'My wife,' he says slowly again, 'has got dementia, just like your Grandma. She's not the same person any more.'

All this time I thought Matt's granddad must be the one with dementia, but that woman I saw . . . the person they go to see . . .

It's his mum.

'Is that why you've been spending so much time with Mum?' I ask.

'What? No! No, I like Sue, of course I do, but it's nothing like that.'

'Oh. It's just, I thought –'

'Oh – no,' he says, smiling. 'We're not in a relationship, Liam. Honestly. I think we both just needed a friend to talk to. It's horrible, when it's someone so close to you. Isabelle looks as beautiful as the day I married her, but inside, she's . . .'

He trails off again and covers his face. His shoulders wobble up and down and he's still covering his eyes and part of me wants to reach out and pat him on the shoulder, but is that normal for a kid and someone else's dad? When he takes his hands away, his eyes are wet.

'She's just not there, Liam. She's not there. It's not her. It's . . .'

'Like there's a demon in her,' I say quietly, 'eating her from the inside out.'

He looks up. 'Yeah. Yes. Like there's a demon.'

37

After school the next day, Matt's waiting by the back fence.

'Why was my dad round your house last night?' he says.

'What?' I try to move past him but he blocks me off.

'Don't play dumb. I thought I told you to make sure your mum stays away from him.' He steps closer. There's no one nearby. Most of the kids have gone home now, and the few that are left are all going out of the main entrance.

'They're not going out,' I say quickly. 'They're just friends.'

'Liar!' he spits, getting right in my face now. 'You and your stories. I know what you did – that night in the road. I know what you did.'

He rocks back and forth on his heels. His eyes are

like Daisy's when she sees a cat in the garden, and he doesn't take them off me.

'I should kill you,' he says.

I step back automatically. *Run* – that's the only thing in my head and it's going round and round as Matt comes closer.

'Do you think I liked being in hospital?' He can't expect an answer because he ploughs straight on: 'A week! Lying there with a broken arm, everyone thinking I'm some kind of muppet who doesn't know how to cross the road. The police came, you know. I could have dobbed you in. I know what you did. It was that thing. That gargoyle. I should kill you!'

Those last words come out in a snarl.

Come on, Liam. Run. But my legs are shaking. They don't feel like mine any more.

'I saw your mum,' I say, just to change the subject.

But it's the wrong thing to say.

It's very much the wrong thing to say, because now he's grabbing my T-shirt and shoving me back, back, back. His nose is big in my face and it wrinkles as he snarls again.

'You what?' he says.

'I – I –'

'I *heard* what you said.'

The words come out in a rush as I try to squirm away. 'I was there visiting my grandma. She's got a demon in her, so I was there to see her and on the way out I saw your mum. I thought it must be your granddad in there because I thought you had to be old to get the disease and everyone in there has it, don't they? But it wasn't your granddad. It was her – I recognized her from the photo. It was your mum . . .'

'What the hell are you talking about? *Demon in her?*'

His grip loosens and I wriggle out and run.

I don't even think about where I'm going – just as long as it's away from him.

Through the gate and across the street and down the alley towards the rec. My footsteps ring off the walls but his are right there too.

Don't look back, I tell myself, *just don't look back*, because in the movies when they do that they always trip and fall and get caught.

Pain stabs my side and I try to ignore it, try to push on.

I'm going to get away. I think I'm going to get away.

Then Matt clips my foot and it drags on the ground and now I'm stumbling. I reach out to steady myself but it's too late. The ground rises up, getting closer and closer to my face and then I'm skidding across the concrete.

The rough ground gouges my skin. My arms and knees are on fire. But I don't have time to look at them because now Matt's on top of me, pinning me to the ground.

'Do *not* run away from me,' he spits. His eyes are wild. I've never seen him like this. 'And if you ever, *ever* say anything about my mum again, you're dead. D'you get me? DEAD!'

I try and shrug him off but he's too heavy.

'I just wanted to – let you know that I – I get it.'

He takes the pressure off my chest. Just a bit, but enough to breathe.

'What?' he says.

'I understand,' I wheeze, gulping in air. 'Well, I don't – not really . . .'

'What are you talking about?'

'I can't remember my Grandma properly. But I've seen what it does to the people who can. The demon in her makes Mum get drunk and it made Jess bunk school. And that makes me sad. So I understand, a bit . . .'

'You don't,' says Matt, in this calm voice that's somehow even scarier than the snarling spitting one.

He climbs off my chest and stands up. At first I don't move, my back's aching too much, my arms are going numb, but he's just standing there, so eventually I sit up.

'No one understands,' he says. 'No one can ever understand.'

But my mind's run off, back to the church, back to the creature I've tried to forget. Maybe Mrs Culpepper *was* trying to tell me something. I can't undo what Stonebird did to Matt that night. But I can try and put things right . . . for him and for me.

One more story . . .

'I thought only old people got demons inside them,' I say, snapping back to Matt's glare. He didn't say anything when I sat up, so I slowly get to my feet. 'I didn't realize you could get one as young as your mum.'

'It's *dementia*,' he says. 'She's not got a demon in her.'

'Well, my sister says Grandma's got a demon inside her, eating her from the inside out. And it's true. I know it's true. I've seen it.'

Matt sighs.

He rests back on the wall, eyes glinting.

'It does look a bit like that, I guess. *Demon in her.*'

'I get what it's like.'

He stands there in silence, head hanging.

'It was her own fault,' he says eventually, in such a tiny voice I barely hear it. 'It was her fault. It was all her fault. She wouldn't. I told her to let go and she wouldn't . . .'

What?

I'm bursting to know more but I don't dare say anything in case he stops.

So I just stand there waiting, looking at the top of Matt's head because he's still staring at the ground. People are walking past us now, on their way to or from the high street, but I ignore them.

'It was a year ago,' he says. 'I bought some water bombs to throw at cars from the tree house, but when she saw them she tried to take them off me. So I snatched them away. She yelled, so I yelled louder, and she yelled even louder, and then she just stopped. She held her heart. She said, *Oh* . . . That's all, just *Oh* . . . and crumpled to the ground. I think it was her heart that did it. Something to do with her heart. But she hit her head. She hit her head and she didn't wake up.'

My mouth is hanging open in the World's Biggest 'O' and it's in capitals because I can't believe what I'm hearing.

'But in the care home, I saw—'

'She's awake now,' he says, reading my mind. 'She woke up after three days. But her memory just got worse and worse. At first she remembered everything, except what had happened to her. But then she started to forget things we'd just told her. Now she tries to give me pocket money a hundred times every visit, even if she's already given me something, even if I show it to her. Sometimes she can't even remember my name.'

After that, the silence is a heavy blanket over the alley. He's just standing there and I'm standing opposite him and I don't know what to do, so I just wait.

'It *was* her fault,' he says, but his voice is weaker this time.

His eyes flare open, stabbing right into me, asking for help.

'It was her fault,' he says again. 'It *was* her fault. It *was*!'

He falls to his knees, looking up at me.

Matt. The hard nut. The same boy who's made my life at this school a living hell.

'But Dad said it was me. He said if I hadn't bought the water bombs then none of this would have happened. He said it was my fault. He said I put her in the care home, that she had a stroke because of me, that she's got dementia because of me.'

'That doesn't sound like him,' I say.

'It was just once, right at the beginning. He was raging. He said sorry for it after, apologized for days, but I can't forget it. He said I stole his wife from him. And I did, didn't I?'

He crawls closer until he's at my feet.

I try and back up, but he keeps coming.

His voice is a slow whine. He's shaking his head, mouth working in silence, and even after everything, even after all I've been through, my gut is squirming.

How can I be feeling sorry for him? For Matt!

He grips my shoes, looking up into my eyes, head shaking.

'I did . . .' he says, over and over. 'I did . . .'

I can't move any further. My back's against the wall.

A million thoughts crash around in my head but one pops up bigger than the rest.

Matt's like Mum. The only difference is he doesn't have anything to take his mind off the demon eating his own mum. That's probably why he's been so angry all this time. It's all bottled up, all the questions and the hatred and the love that's never going to be the same again. All the memories and dreams. All of it is bottled up inside him and shaken up like a can of Coke, fizzing and foaming and desperate to burst.

I crouch down too, ignoring my stinging knees. I stare straight into his eyes.

'It wasn't your fault,' I say. Part of me thinks that's a lie. But the other part of me says, *Imagine if you were in his shoes.* So I do imagine it, and I don't get it, don't get how he can still be human and go to school and do all that normal stuff when his Mum's been taken away from him.

'It was,' he says, sniffing. 'It was. It was.'

He's quiet after that.

So I say them. I say the words that are burning in the back of my mind.

'I think I know something that can help.'

38

Here's the plan:

- Wait until the bell goes at quarter past three.
- Hide in school until the class is empty.
- Very Important: wait until Mrs Culpepper has gone home.
- Borrow the magic egg (it's not stealing because we'll put it back).
- Go to the church and tell a story.

I know I said I wouldn't tell any more stories about Stonebird, but I've got an idea. And if it works, it might be able to help Mum as well as Matt.

Everything goes smoothly to start with. We have maths, which I manage to stay awake for, and English, and in history we learn about a new war hero called Charles Coward, who is my favourite so far because he totally wasn't a coward. Then Mrs Culpepper tells us to form a circle and she goes over to her desk and takes out the magic egg from the drawer on the right.

'I hope you've all been thinking about your stories,' she says, holding the egg in her hand.

Matt's staring at the egg and you can practically hear his mind whirring. As Mrs Culpepper walks over to the circle I try and sneak a look at the drawer.

It doesn't have a lock . . .

Matt gives me a knowing look that shows he's seen it too.

My lips twitch in a smile but I look away quickly.

The corners of my mouth feel numb because I haven't smiled in so long. And smiling with Matt? Too weird.

The egg goes round the circle and the stories flow and I know it's getting warmer and warmer. When it comes to me, I just make something up about Daisy getting chased by a pig out in the fields, and then pass it on.

And soon enough the bell goes.

My eyes dart to the clock and see the hands at three fifteen. The hairs on my neck shoot up and it feels like they're wriggling.

It's time.

I take ages packing my stuff away as the class empties around me. Chairs scrape and bang, feet pound the floor as everyone rushes out into the hall. Mrs Culpepper stays behind and soon it's just her and me and Matt and his friends. She puts the egg back in the drawer and starts to tidy her desk.

Matt and his mates get up to go, and then it's only me left in the room. I sling my bag over my shoulder and walk out, with Mrs Culpepper smiling behind me.

'Look who's all on his own,' says a voice from the corner of the hall, by the coat hooks.

It's Joe. He cracks his knuckles with a loud snap, like bone breaking in two. This is one of those cartoon moments where I should gulp a really loud gulp and run off. But instead I freeze as he lurches towards me. Matt and Cheesy are waiting by the door. I cast Matt a nervous glance, but he doesn't see.

'I don't think I've ever properly thanked you for what you did to us,' says Joe. As he gets closer he seems to grow, until he's twice my size, towering over me with his huge hands forming giant fists.

Electricity jolts through my legs.

Run!

I'm just about to peg it when Matt clears his throat.

'Oi, Joe,' he says. 'Leave it. Come on – there'll be a chance for that later.'

Joe throws a quick look over his shoulder. 'What?'

'I said, leave it!'

Joe turns back to me, glaring. I can see it in his eyes – he wants to charge, he wants to smack me one for scaring him with Stonebird. He takes another step closer, practically drooling.

'*Joe!*' says Matt sternly.

He stops and turns around. Matt's shoulders slump just slightly, like he's breathing a sigh of relief, and then he's gone, and Cheesy and Joe are following him out of the door.

Matt and I had said we'd meet by the climbing frame at half three, but first I need to hide on my own, because Matt has to shake off the others.

I lock myself in the loo again, the same one Matt tried to smash down, and imagine the minutes ticking by on my broken watch.

Will it work? Can it possibly work? Two kids and an egg and a whole lot of luck.

I wait until I can't take the tension any more, then sneak out round the back in case Mrs Culpepper's still around. I can't let her see me . . . If she knows I was hanging around the classroom she might get suspicious when the egg goes missing.

There's a side door out of the school behind the Year Four bookshelves. It's one of those fire-exit doors with the metal bar you have to push to open, so it's easy to get out. It leads out to the pond, where –

I shake away the image of falling in.

After that it's the big playground, where the bank of grass is, with a climbing frame at the back near the hedge. A big hill blocks the playground from view. Matt's not there yet, so I crouch low and wait.

It's so quiet that every sound seems louder. My heart. The insects humming. The birds tweeting and singing in the trees. A plane roars overhead, leaving a white trail through the blue sky.

'Boo!'

I jump, scrambling to my feet.

Matt staggers back laughing, covering his mouth to try to keep quiet.

'That's not funny,' I say, but I can't help smiling.

'How long do we wait?' he says.

My watch is still cracked, so I check the sky to try and guess how much daylight we have left. 'Thirty minutes,' I guess. 'It should get a bit darker then.'

'Cover of darkness. Like it,' he says.

The sun dips lower in the sky, painting a line of orange above the trees to our right. My breath starts to cloud in front of me and I have to rub my arms against the cold. School jumpers are warm, but not *that* warm.

Matt hops to his feet. 'Let's go, before I freeze my nuts off,' he says.

Dim light shines from some of the windows in the school, but most of it is in darkness. Probably cleaners or teachers staying late. There are no lights on in the Year Six classroom, which means Mrs Culpepper must have left.

Across the grass, towards the flint wall and the door to the hall.

We sneak up to the classroom door and peer in.

'Wait!' Matt whispers furiously, pointing up. A red light flashes inside the room from a white box on the wall. 'A sensor,' he says.

'Will an alarm go off?'

'I hope not . . .' He sighs. 'Not much we can do now, I guess. We'll have to be quick.'

He opens the door, and just like that we're in.

'Get your egg. I'll keep watch.'

The red light flashes every time I move, and at first I freeze.

Come on, Liam, come on . . .

Flash flash flash flash. Even my breathing makes

it flicker, and if it is turned on then the police have probably got the message already and all I'm doing is standing around waiting.

Taking a deep breath, I run over to Mrs Culpepper's desk and open the drawer –

But the egg's not there.

She's taken it home!

She can't have. She wouldn't! I saw her put it in the drawer.

Flash flash flash flash.

My palms grow slick with sweat as I rummage through the other drawers, lifting up papers and moving books, just praying I'll find it, but it's not here, it's not anywhere, it's –

It's there. In the bottom drawer.

She must have got it out again and moved it after school. The egg's cold in my hand. The stories have all seeped away, and the warmth has gone with them.

Flash flash flash flash.

'Come *on*!' Matt hisses urgently from the door.

'Got it,' I say, running back to him.

'Nice. Let's go.'

The cleaner comes round the corner just as we close the door behind us. 'And what do we have here?' he says in a strong syrupy accent.

'Just two kids on their way to church,' Matt calls over his shoulder.

He runs off laughing, and I run with him, heart pounding, stomach squeezed tight with the thrill of it, because we so nearly got caught and maybe we did get caught because the cleaner could tell on us and then the game will be up.

But who cares? We're putting the plan into action tonight.

And if it works, nothing else will matter tomorrow.

39

Night falls quickly as we make our way to the church. Bats fly above the long, dark drive, swooping over the lumpy graveyard and swirling around the crumbling building.

I'm halfway towards the entrance when I realize Matt's not following me.

'I'm not going in,' he says, eyes darting around the grounds.

'It's not really haunted. They're just stories.'

'Yeah, I know. I'm not scared. It's just . . .'

'The gargoyle?'

He nods. Thin shadows from the bare trees move across his face. Part of me doesn't want to go in either. The thought of Stonebird's bloodstained clawed hands makes me feel sick. And what if it doesn't work? What if we've done all this for nothing?

'I'll see you in a minute,' I say.

The egg's colder than ever in my hand and I'm thinking, *It's not going to work, there's only one of you, not a whole class, it'll never get warm enough*, and, *It won't work it won't work it won't work*. But it's *got* to work. It's got to.

Through the crumbling door and across the flagstone floor, with my footsteps echoing in the emptiness and the moonlight glinting from the broken glass in the windows, and the cold cold cold of the church pressing all around me.

The crypt door swings open easily and there inside it, sitting in the dark, is Stonebird. His tail is curled around his feet and his wings are folded and he's resting his great glaring head in a huge clawed hand.

And his eyes . . .

Don't think about the eyes.

I hold the egg in both hands and rub it to try to warm it up, but it's cold, so cold.

Think, Liam, think . . .

With my eyes closed I can picture Matt falling to his knees in front of me, desperate. I can see his mum whispering to herself, on her own in the care home all because she banged her head. I can see Jess watching as Grandma eats her drawing and Mum leaning in close, gripping her hand, trying to find the person inside the ancient body, trying to fight off the demon.

I stand there holding the egg thinking these things, and I tell a story.

And the story I tell is this.

There's a gargoyle hidden deep in the haunted church.

It sits in the cold and the dark, waiting. It's waited for so long that it can no longer remember home.

It sits, and it waits, and it remembers.

Because memories are all it has, when it's alone in the darkness of the crypt. Memories of castles and battles and demons. Memories of all of it, but especially the demons, because that's what gargoyles do, isn't it?

They fight demons.

They protect.

That's why you see them guarding the most important places in the world.

That's why it came here, isn't it? To protect.

The egg's getting warmer. I can feel it, feel it spreading through my hands and fingers, and maybe I'm just imagining it but it feels alive, like it's writhing, like the surface of the egg is shifting in my hands.

It protected the kid who needed saving.

But that kid doesn't need protecting. His grandma does. And Matt's mum. And all the people in the care

262

home who have to fight the demon every single day just to remember their life.

It's those people who need help.

The gargoyle has not heard of this particular demon before. But it knows where to go, and it spreads its huge wings and takes off into the night, flies through the village until he gets to the care home. And –

A noise makes me stop.

A crunching, shifting, grinding noise. My eyes burst open but Stonebird hasn't moved. He's just sitting there, a statue covered in shadows, watching. Always watching.

'*Please,*' I say. '*Please help them. Please go to them.*'

The egg's hot in my hands now.

I don't remember walking forward, but now I'm right in front of him, looking up into his stone face and his stone eyes and reaching out to touch his stone heart, and it's warm. The grey stone is warm beneath my fingers, as warm as Mrs Culpepper's magic egg.

'They need you,' I say, to the shadows and the silence. 'The demon's real. It's the most real thing in the world. And it's eating them, every bit of them that makes them human. It's ripping them apart and turning them into nothing, just skin and bone and an empty head and eyes that try desperately to remember but don't know how.'

Still nothing.

Why isn't it working?

I've got the egg and I've told a story and it's supposed to work! He's supposed to come alive. Matt's outside and Mum will be wondering where I am, and even if she doesn't know it, she's depending on me, they're all depending on me, and I've failed them.

Because look at him. He's just stone.

Fire rages up inside me and I thump Stonebird hard and feel numbness spreading in my hands where the pain flares, but I block it out because it's nothing, it's not important; the only thing that matters is the story and Stonebird isn't listening.

'Please,' I say, thumping thumping thumping.

Please . . .

Red. I'm bleeding, but I don't even feel it. My blood is on Stonebird's thick, powerful chest where I've been smacking him. Dark patches on the grey stone. Except it's not grey stone. Not any more. Blue veins run through his chest, like the ones in the egg.

What . . . ?

I step back. The veins are writhing in his skin. Wriggling.

Move! Please move!

I close my eyes and picture Grandma and Mum and Matt and his family and all of them, all the people the demon has hurt, and the tears flood down my face.

I don't know how long I stand there, but after a while I remember Matt keeping guard outside, and guilt stabs my insides.

I open my eyes.

Then I blink, and realize what I'm looking at.

Or rather what I'm *not* looking at. Because the crypt's empty.

Stonebird's gone.

40

After lunch the next day, the headmistress calls me into her office. I sit down opposite her and my heart's hammering. The cleaner must have reported us. What if she knows I took the egg? The silence stretches, and I'm thinking, *She knows she knows she knows . . .*

'Your mother just phoned,' she says finally, looking at me over the top of her glasses.

'I'm sorry, Liam, but something's happened at the care home. Your mother wants you to be there. She's coming to pick you up now.'

'What?' *Something's happened?* That could mean anything. What if it's gone wrong? What if Stonebird attacked Grandma like it attacked Matt?

No no no no no . . .

'I'm sure it's nothing to worry about,' she says, in

the kind of voice that doesn't make it any better at all. Teachers are masters of that voice, I reckon. I ask her what, what's going on, what's happened? But she doesn't say any more, just tells me to go and wait for Mum outside in the playground and she'll let Mrs Culpepper know.

The care home's practically empty, apart from the old people shuffling around. It reminds me of that game you can get called Dead Rising. It's this zombie outbreak game where you're trapped in a shopping centre and there are thousands of zombies wandering round and you can break into the shops to get weapons to fight them with, like bowling balls and lawnmowers and golf clubs.

Shuffling and moaning. The smell of burnt meat wafting from the kitchen. You can tell the ones who have been living with a demon for a long time, because their eyes are blank and they stop every now and then looking lost, or groan at you, or say things like, 'You should have seen my prize-winning goats of '98,' and, 'I never can remember how I invented the moon,' and, 'There's a monster on the roof, you know. I dreamed about it last night.'

That one makes me stop, but Mum grabs my hand

and hurries us along the corridor. My shoes squeak on the polished floor as we round the corner towards Grandma's room.

'Wait till you see,' she says. She's said it the whole way here and she's still saying it all the way up to the door. 'Jess is already in there. Wait till you see!'

Mum shoves open the door, and there she is, there's Grandma, sitting up in bed with the sun shining on her face through the open window and the fresh air flowing through and taking the old musty smell with it.

'Liam!' she says, as soon as she sees me.

What?

My feet stop.

She smiles and beckons with her thin bony hand. It doesn't have food on it today –

It's clean and white as she curls her finger to call me over. I check Mum's face in surprise but she just nods and pushes me gently forward.

'My, how you've grown,' says Grandma.

Her eyes are bright and blue and shining and they're surrounded by smiley wrinkles and they don't drift closed every few seconds. All the grey and gloom has gone from the room, blasted out by fresh air and flowers.

'I can't believe it!' she says. 'Come closer and give your Grandma a kiss.'

I automatically check her face but there's no food, no muck, just white wrinkly skin. I bend down and kiss her and she kisses me. When I pull back she reaches out and clutches my hand. Her grip's so strong that my fingers turn white too. I squeeze her hand back.

Mum and Jess are behind me. Warmth comes off them in waves. But I can't take my eyes off Grandma. I stare into her happy blue eyes, trying to find the demon, trying to see if it's in there, but there's only cleverness and stories and jokes waiting to be told. And memories. So many memories.

'Such a handsome one, this,' she says, winking at Mum. 'You'll have the girls chasing after you when you get older. How old are you now?'

'Eleven.'

'Double digits! Eleven is a brilliant age. My, they do grow up fast, don't they?'

She turns to look out of the window. People are sitting out in the sun on benches and their laughter flows through into the room. *Laughter!*

'Do you know,' says Grandma, 'I was just telling Jess – I wouldn't mind going outside for a bit. Do you think we could manage it?'

She tries to get up, her thin arms struggling with the effort, then falls back on to the bed. There's nothing to her, no muscle, just bone with skin hanging from it like a tent without pegs.

'I'll try to find a wheelchair,' Mum says.

I bend down and give Grandma my shoulder to lean on. She grips my arm and wobbles with the pressure as she tries again to climb over the railing on the bed.

'It's like they think we'll escape,' she says, chuckling despite the strain.

Mum comes back with a wheelchair and Jess and I help Grandma into it. She lands with a thud and for a second I think she's hurt herself, but she only slaps the sides with her wrinkled hands.

'Let's have it then,' she says, grinning.

We're laughing as we wheel her out, out into the sunny garden. Laughing like loons. Laughing like we've never laughed before.

41

'Aren't I the lucky lady?' Grandma says, when we help her back into bed. 'It's not every day you get an adventure like that.'

Her eyes . . . they're dancing. It's so easy to see the recognition in them. She's still shrunken and skinny, but somehow she's fuller, more alive.

One of the nurses brings in a pot of tea, and we sit there drinking and talking and eating the leftover chocolates from Grandma's birthday.

'Eighty-six,' she says. 'Fancy that.'

'We found your diary,' Jess says.

'Oh, you did, eh? And I suppose you read it too.'

Mum grins. 'I think she's itching to ask you about Rupert.' Then she whispers, 'She's got a boyfriend herself.'

'*Mum!*'

'Is that right?' says Grandma. 'And when am I going to meet him?'

They start talking about boys, laughing over old stories and mushy details. After a while I step back towards the edge of the room. They don't see me going. They're too interested in their conversation. And I don't blame them.

You know how something can be so amazing or such fun or so unbelievable that you think you're dreaming? And you're scared to pinch yourself because if it is a dream then you don't want to wake up?

That's how I'm feeling now.

I don't want to pinch myself and I'm not going to pinch myself, but there is something that I do want to do.

I slip out of the door and into the hall.

Old men and women pass me by, and nurses too, walking to the common room where I can hear the distant sounds of a TV in the background.

It doesn't take long for me to find the room I'm looking for.

I hesitate for a second, listening for any sound. Will Matt's mum be any better, like Grandma is? If not, I don't know what I'll do. Nothing I say can make it any better. Matt will probably want to kill me all over again.

The door's open, just a crack, but enough for me to see into the room.

Matt's there. And Gary too. They're sitting around the bed, sitting around Matt's mum, and although I can't hear what they're saying, I can tell one thing.

They're smiling.

'Here he is,' says Grandma, when I make my way back to her room.

She calls me over, and I sit beside her on the bed.

'You know what?' she says to Mum. 'I'd love another cuppa.'

Mum stands up and gives Jess a look that says, *Follow me*, and they both head out of the room, leaving me on my own with Grandma.

I know Grandma's only done it so I can have my own time with her. There are so many things I want to ask, but now the moment's come everything's bubbling up at once and I don't know what to say.

'I hear you're looking after your mother,' she says.

'Yeah.'

'And your sister too?'

'Trying to,' I say.

'I bet she gives you hell, eh?'

A smile creeps on to my face. 'Sometimes.'

We're quiet for a while. Her eyes are so bright. You can tell they've seen so many things, but even so they're the youngest part of her face. Looking at them, I can almost see the thirteen-year-old girl I've been reading about in her diary.

'It's not just me though,' I say.

'No.'

She knows. I can tell she knows.

I feel in my pocket for the egg, and take it out. As soon as Grandma sees it, her eyes light up. 'Ah,' she says. 'Yes. It's been a long time since . . . I've seen this.'

'Mrs Culpepper gave it to me,' I say, and I know it's a lie, but Mrs Culpepper did warn me that she was leaving, so maybe she wanted me to take it.

'Of course. And so it comes full circle, eh?'

'Is it true?' I ask her.

Her eyebrows shoot up. 'Is what true?'

'Did Stonebird really follow you from Notre Dame?'

She smiles, showing her false teeth. 'It's true if you want it to be.'

I don't really know what to say to that, so I think of another question that's been on my mind, and try and find a way to word it so she can't answer in riddles.

'Grandma?'

'Yes, pet?'

274

'What happened on 16 January?'

'Oh,' she says. 'That. You're a clever one, aren't you?'

Something flickers in her eyes. I can't stop thinking that she did it, she killed that girl, or at least she asked Stonebird to – which is the same thing really. My throat tightens and I want to step back, I want to leave, but I can't. I have to know.

'You can take that look off your face, mind.'

When I swallow, it's loud in my ears.

'You're wondering if your poor old Grandma had it in her to murder a schoolgirl?'

'It's just that – well, you said . . .'

Grandma taps the side of her head. 'Dementia,' she says. 'It's a nasty thing. Once it gets a grip on you, it doesn't let go. Makes you say things that never ought to be said. Makes you say things that aren't you at all.'

But she must recognize the look on my face, because then she says, 'I'll tell you what. You have a dig in that cupboard there, and see if you can't find my sketchbook. I know it's here somewhere, because I was showing it off to the nurses last night.'

'You've got your sketchbook here?'

'Of course! Where else would it be?'

I shift off the side of the bed and open the cupboard. There's a DVD player and a CD player and a few old birthday cards, and there's a box that looks like it might have jewellery inside. And there, at the back, is a black leather sketchbook.

'That's the ticket,' Grandma says, as I bring it over to her.

She flicks through drawing after drawing – some of Paris and some of the countryside and there are loads of gravestones and gargoyles. Then she stops and holds a page up to me. At first I don't really get it. There's a girl, which I guess must be her, but around her it's a mess of black. And shielding her head with its wings is –

'Stonebird,' I whisper.

'Now,' Grandma says, 'you pass that egg here. I'll tell you a story.'

42

'There was a girl who came to Swanbury during the War,' she says.

'You.'

'Of course me. Now keep quiet for a moment, will you? Didn't Mrs Culpepper teach you not to talk when you don't have the egg?'

'Sorry,' I say quickly, but she grins to let me know she's joking.

'I didn't think I'd be in Swanbury for very long. Paris was our home. We moved there so my father could take over the family business. And you have to remember, back then people said the War would be over by Christmas. It wasn't. Days became weeks and weeks turned into months, and the lady I was living with, dear Mrs Woods, decided I'd better start going to school.

'As I'm sure you know, it can be a bit horrible, moving schools. If you try too hard, they'll be on you. If you don't try at all, they'll think you're some kind of hopeless case. And if you're too good at something – well – bully for you. Quite literally, in my case.'

The graveyard flashes in my mind, the headstone with Claire's name on it.

'Claire didn't take well to my joining her class. She picked on me, called me names, put things in my hair and chocolate on my seat so it would melt all over my skirt. Then it got worse. They had this ritual, you see. Even in those days the church was haunted. People thought it was anyway, and that's as good as the real thing half the time. They used to dare each other to go in there at night, then shut them in. See how long it took for them to come banging on the door in terror.'

It's all so similar to Matt and his mates. They never tried to lock me in the church, but it wouldn't have surprised me if they had. It's not that far from dumping me in a pond or chasing me around school.

But I've never wanted to kill them. Hurt them, maybe, but never kill them.

'Naturally Claire came after me. She chased me into the church. I tried to fight her off, and that's when I heard it – a deep, thunderous crack and a rumble so loud you'd have thought we were getting bombed. We were both frozen in shock as the stones fell.'

Grandma stops talking, her face frozen, staring into the distance.

'What happened?' I whisper, leaning closer. 'How did you get out?'

'Thankfully Stonebird wasn't quite as slow as I was. As the roof split open, he dived in, plunged down and covered us with his huge wings. The stones crashed against him. The noise was hellacious. I've never seen his eyes burn as bright as they did that night. Flames of pure gold they were. But Claire didn't realize he was protecting us. A gargoyle moving? You can imagine the look on her face. It wasn't far to the door. I could see the cogs whirring in her brain. *Get down*, I said, *get down*, but she wouldn't listen. She ran. She ran, that foolish girl, and it was the last thing she did.'

I realize I'm holding my breath and let it out slowly. She's telling the truth. Or at least I think she is. But part of me still believes that all stories are lies, and if that's true then how do you know what's real and what's not?

'You were wondering what happened on 16 January, Liam. You were wondering if I killed Claire Smith. Well, that's what happened. You can decide for yourself how to feel about it. Goodness knows I'm not sure what to think, even after all these years. I just try to forget it. Which was easy, until today.'

'It was an accident,' I say. 'It was just a horrible accident. You're not a killer at all.'

She smiles, and her eyes crinkle around the edges. 'Maybe. But I might have been able to do more. And isn't that the same thing?'

'No,' I say. 'I don't think so.'

All this time I thought Grandma used Stonebird to kill that girl. You can't control him, not properly, and I know how easy it is to go too far. I made a mistake with Matt because I was angry and upset, and he broke his arm. It could have been a lot worse.

But Grandma isn't a killer. I should never have suspected her.

'Does it ever get any easier?' I say. 'Moving, I mean.'

'Oh yes.' She winks and rubs my arm with her wrinkly hand. 'I think you know it does. Here, look, we've got company again. And tea! I love a good cuppa.'

Later that evening, when we get in the car to leave, I poke my head out of the window and look up, and he's there. I can see him, keeping watch on the roof.

The dark shape of Stonebird, crouching in the shadows.

43

'It worked,' Matt says excitedly, rushing up to me at the school gates. 'It bleeding worked! You did it!'

'*We* did it.'

Matt grins, and I smile right back.

'Have you got the egg?' he says.

I hold it out to him. The warmth of the story has long since vanished.

'Mrs Culpepper didn't even look for it yesterday,' he says. 'I guess she didn't want to do the story circle without you there. If you put it back this morning, she won't even know it was gone.' He glances up and spots Cheesy and Joe lurking at the edge of the playground. 'Better go and meet up with them lot,' he says. 'See you in class!'

Apparently the human body is sixty-per-cent water.

But right now I feel more like sixty-per-cent balloons, as if I'm floating up and up and up. I can't take the smile off my face.

Grandma's had a demon in her for so long that I couldn't remember her from before, but now I don't need to. First I had the diary, then I got to speak to her, properly speak to her, and the whole time she was completely back to her old self.

And Mum – it seems like she's really been trying hard to stay happy. But staying happy must be impossible when Grandma's so ill.

Once, five years ago, Daisy ran away and I thought I'd never see her again because there was no sign of her for sixteen days and thirteen hours. But then one day there was a knock on the door and there she was. The woman who brought her back moaned about how she turned up in their garden wrecking the bins. But her voice was drowned out by the electric sparks of happiness surging through my body as Daisy wagged her tail and barked and bounded into my arms.

Mum must feel a bit like that, but a million times more, because even though Daisy is my best friend, she's still just a dog. And Mum's got her own mum back.

I'm so lost in thought walking into school that I don't notice the signs that something's wrong.

The first thing is the quiet.

Our class is never this quiet in the morning.

Halfway to the desk, I see the second sign.

'Where's Mrs Culpepper?' I ask the teacher who is not Mrs Culpepper.

She has her back to me at first, but as she turns her face tightens and her eyes shrink to points.

'You're *late*,' she says. 'Sit down, please, and don't disturb my class again.'

But I don't sit down. I blink, taking it all in, her ragged face and her scraggly grey hair and the class all around me sitting still as statues, not daring to move.

'Where's Mrs Culpepper?' I say again, panic rising in me.

'She's gone,' she says simply. 'I'm afraid you'll have to put up with me now.'

A whisper beside me: 'Sit down, Liam!' But I ignore it. Something rises inside me, something raw and fiery and real. I don't know what it is, but what I do know is I'm not sitting down. Not here. Not for her.

'Sit down, boy,' the woman says again.

'*Where – is – Mrs – Brown?*' I say, loud and slow.

Her face is white and strained and there are no smiles in her eyes.

She reaches out to grab me. I yank my arm free but I'm still holding the marble egg and it slips out of my hand.

It falls in slow motion . . .

It hits the ground hard.

It cracks in two.

Everyone in the class gasps when they realize what's happened. All I can think is, *How is this happening, how is this happening how, how, how –?* The teacher steps back and in that moment of distraction a sudden thought catches fire in my mind.

I run.

Out through the door and across the hall and into the playground. Because Mrs Culpepper's gone. Her egg is broken. And if the egg's broken, my connection to Stonebird might be too.

Please be there.

The thought pounds in my head.

Please, please be there.

Sweat runs into my eyes and I rub at them with my sleeve, stumbling on.

But I don't stop and don't care as long as I'm moving.

On and on and on and on until my legs buckle. Pain lances through my stomach and I clench my side trying to get rid of the stitch, knowing that I need to keep moving. My legs are jelly. I can't feel them any more, but I will them to move.

When I can't run, I walk, dragging myself forward.

Panting heavily, I force myself on until I get to the care home. My legs finally give out and I tumble down on to the rough concrete. The pavement rips at my palms. It stings where it takes the skin off. But I push myself up because I need to see . . .

No.

No.

The roof's empty.

Stonebird has gone.

44

I just stand there, gulping air, my jumper damp and clinging to me.

Blood pounds in my ears.

Gone.

He's gone.

And that means . . .

I run up to the door and dial the number on the keypad. The receptionist doesn't give me a second glance as I run past, but all the old people turn to watch me charge down the corridor and round the corner and up to Grandma's door.

Mum's inside when I get there. I barge in and she jumps out of the chair.

'Liam? What are you *doing* here? I thought you were at school!'

Her cheeks are red and wet streaks run down them on to her chin. I look past her towards Grandma, but Mum grabs my shoulders and shakes her head. More tears run down and I can see she's trying to fight it, trying to hold it in, but once they start they just run and run and run.

'Liam, pet . . . she's not in good shape,' she says, eyes shining wet.

I shrug her off. 'I want to see her!'

I fight my way past, but Grandma's eyes are staring at the ceiling, seeing things that I can't. Her mouth opens and closes, forming the shapes of words, but she's not speaking.

'Grandma? Grandma, it's me. Liam.'

She reaches out to touch my face, but Mum pulls me back.

'It's best not to get too close,' she says.

My mouth hangs open and I try to close it but it just drops uselessly again. Words form in my mind but they're distant, and when I try and grab them and use them they vanish. A shiver runs through me, and not because I'm cold.

The demon. It's back. It's back worse than ever . . .

But even as I think it, I know I'm wrong. Grandma's eyes are empty. There's not even that fire in there any more. They're windows on to nothing. She's a husk. The demon hasn't just come back. It's been and eaten everything and gone already.

And left us with this.

Yesterday Grandma was laughing and smiling and winking and telling stories. Now she can barely move.

It's not fair.

I don't understand how this can happen, how people can have a heartbeat and a mind and be looking right at you but not really be there at all.

But I guess that's all we are, isn't it? Memories. Just a load of memories rolled up into a person. And when they go, we're left with nothing.

45

'Do you know,' says Mum, hours later, 'your grandma kept saying the strangest things today.'

We're lying on the sofa, Mum, Jess and me, lying and holding each other and listening to the quiet of the evening as the room gets darker around us and the fire burns low and orange, giving out its warmth.

'She kept talking about a monster on the roof . . .'

Jess frowns. 'Weird,' she says.

'I know. But she was convinced, she really was.'

'You're talking about her like she's dead,' I say.

'Oh, Liam, dear . . .' She pauses, and the pause feels like a hammer getting ready to slam. 'I don't think it's going to be long.'

We don't talk much after that.

I close my eyes and I keep hearing Mrs Culpepper

saying, *Happy memories are powerful things*, so in my head I run through all the stories I've read in Grandma's diary.

She liked art and racing cars and flowers and walks in the sun and feeling the sand between her toes and having the same birthday as the Queen.

She liked all of those things and so much more and now no one will ever know, because she can't remember.

When I was at my old school and Rory Summers died in a fire one night, they called a special assembly in the morning and brought in the village vicar and he read from the Bible and told stories and said Rory will live on forever in our hearts. And I thought, *What a load of rubbish.*

You don't remember things with your heart.

You remember things with your head. And you can't remember things forever. I know that to be one-hundred-per-cent true because I've seen the demon rip every last memory out of Grandma and now she remembers nothing. And if it happened to Grandma, it could happen to me too.

You can't remember things forever.

But you can try.

Rory will live on in my head, and Grandma will too. And even if the demon comes to visit me when I'm older,

I'll find a way to beat it. I'll write in my notebook every day about all the things that Grandma liked.

'I'll remember her,' I say.

Mum squeezes my shoulder to say, *Thank you*, and Jess holds my hand, and we sit like that until it gets dark, just the three of us, with Daisy snoring quietly at our feet.

46

Grandma dies two days later.

One minute she's breathing wheezily, her tiny body rising and falling – and then she stops. I've never seen a dead body before. So still. So sudden. My stomach drops, and I clench my jaw, force myself to stay strong.

Mum's there at her bedside, her face wrinkled up and crying quietly. Jess and I hug her from both sides. Mum wipes her cheeks with a tissue that's starting to fall apart.

'I think –' says Mum, drawing a raggedy breath – 'I think it's probably for the best.'

Grandma's face looks whiter than ever against the blue bed sheets.

Her claw-like hand is still gripping Mum's.

I can't take my eyes off Grandma's fingers. All those

diary entries, all those drawings. They're never going to move again.

Finally Mum lets go of Grandma's hand. She rests it carefully on the duvet.

And we just stand there in silence, none of us wanting to turn away.

The funeral's at the haunted church. It was a special request in Grandma's will. And you'll never guess who comes.

Matt.

He's there with his dad. But get this. His mum's there too. She's dressed in a white top and grey skirt and black jacket. A twinge of jealousy flickers for a moment because *how can she be standing here when Grandma's getting lowered into the cold dirt*, but I force it away because I can see how happy they are. I mean, they're sad – everyone's sad because it's a funeral – but they're leaning together and smiling at each other. When Matt sees me looking, he walks over to say hi, and even though he's trying to look solemn, his eyes are shining with happiness.

'I'm so sorry, mate,' he says. 'I really mean it.'

'It's OK,' I say, even though it's not OK, it's not OK at all, because Grandma's dead and it was all for nothing.

No, not for nothing.

Matt's mum looks over and smiles, the sun bouncing off her golden hair.

Not for nothing . . .

'How—' I start to say, but Matt cuts me off.

'No one knows. Doctors are calling it a miracle. And that's what it is, isn't it?' he says, nudging me again. 'A miracle from that gargoyle of yours.'

I picture Mrs Culpepper telling her story.

Her eyes, looking at me over the egg.

So make use of it while you can . . .

'Where is it, anyway?' says Matt. 'The gargoyle.'

'Dunno.'

'We're missing you at school. Mrs Culpepper's still not back, but at least we got them to fire old Miss Farrow. Absolutely *bonkers* she was. She talked rubbish too. The head gave a talk in assembly about Mrs Culpepper. It was her mum, just like she said. She had to go up to look after her.'

'I hope she doesn't have a demon in her,' I say.

I hope she's got Stonebird there to look after her.

And thinking that, I know she does.

After they lower Grandma's body into the ground, the vicar asks if anyone would like to say anything. No one steps forward, so Mum wipes her eyes and raises her hand.

'I will,' she says, walking up to the table that's set out by the grave. There are flower petals for people to scatter on the coffin, and a pile of mud to dig into and sprinkle over it too.

Mum grabs some petals and turns to face the crowd.

She opens her mouth, but nothing comes out. Her eyes are wide and brimming with tears, and she looks from face to face until the tears start flowing. Then she looks down at the petals in her hand and back up again, at Jess and me and the family members we haven't seen for years.

'I –' says Mum.

And she cries quietly into the wind and the rustle of the scratchy bare trees.

'I'll say something,' says a small voice.

And then I realize the voice came from me.

I blink and look around and everyone's staring and some people are smiling encouragingly, and one old woman with a big nose says, *Oh, how sweet*, but it sounds distant, a dream of a dream.

My feet carry me over to Mum and she wipes her eyes and hugs me and says, *Thank you*, in this quiet, quiet voice, then goes back to take her place in the crowd.

The faces stare. The vicar clears his throat.

The petals lift in the gentle breeze and dance along the table.

A quick flicker of movement catches my eye. Over by the church. There's something there, on the roof. It's leaning forward, resting on its hand, watching.

Stonebird.

It's got to be Stonebird.

With a sudden surge of excitement, I turn back to Matt, and he's grinning this big grin that lets me know he can see it too.

When I first heard about Grandma's dementia, I used to think that there was no point in living, because no matter what you did, you'd just forget about it.

But I don't think that's true any more. Grandma might have forgotten everything about herself, but that doesn't mean we have. All it means is that it's down to us to remember her. It doesn't make her life pointless – it makes it even more important.

I grab a handful of petals and stare down at them, thinking about Grandma.

And I tell one more story. But it's not about Stonebird this time.

It's about her.

So everyone here will know her. Really know her.

And remember.

My Grandma liked art and racing cars and flowers and walks in the sun and feeling the sand between her toes and having the same birthday as the Queen . . .

ACKNOWLEDGEMENTS

This book wouldn't be the thing you are holding today without the help of some remarkable people. A huge, heartfelt thank-you to:

Gemma Cooper, my agent, who saw *Stonebird* when it was no more than a one-sentence idea and was there every step of the way.

Sarah Lambert, my editor, whose vision and passion I'm still in awe of, and the whole brilliant team at Quercus.

Talya Baker, who made me look cleverer than I am.

And, lastly, I'd like to thank J. K. Rowling, for showing me the magic of reading when I was Liam's age.